JOLLY

JOLLY

By JOHN WESTON

DAVID McKAY COMPANY, INC.
NEW YORK

JOLLY

LIBRARY OF CONGRESS CATALOG CARD NUMBER: 65-12265

MANUFACTURED IN THE UNITED STATES OF AMERICA

VAN REES PRESS • NEW YORK

for Jane

This story is fictional as are all its characters and situations

JOLLY

ONE

JOLLY shifted the girl to the edge of his lap, against the door, and leaned over her legs and with the sleeve of his Levi jacket wiped away the steam that had formed on the windshield. As the glass came clear the spring moon jumped forward white and black and seemed to slope from where they sat, four in the front seat of the Blue Goose, down the graveled road for perhaps fifty feet until the road curved and then straight ahead across the slight mounds, stopping to reflect on the sparse markers and the still sparser flat, bright headstones. Two hundred feet beyond, the light was broken by a wide dark strip whose shape undulated from somewhere among the pines to the left and disappeared among similar pines a long way to the right. That would be the granite wall. Peculiarly and ridiculously shaped, it swung with grim merriment along the border of the graveyard, six feet high in the middle of the swing, swooping to twelve feet at the highest points. Beyond that, unseen, lay the paved road that ran out into the country one way and back through Shaker Village and on into town the other.

His eyes swept all this and came back to rove among the mounds and markers. A shudder passed from between his shoulders to the small of his back, which could have been caused by the edge of winter around the car, or from the heat of four experimenting bodies inside, or from something that had lain below the surface of his consciousness for a long time. Jolly himself took it as a sign of relief. Although he had never before been there at night, the scene was unchanged from the way he remembered it the first time he had seen it seven years ago when he was nine. He knew that if he cleared the right-hand window beyond the girl's shoulder, he would see the mausoleum standing nerveless and enduring as it always had. Jolly did not want to disturb the girl, whose mouth had come to rest at last with her face, against the inside curve of his arm. His eyes squinted slightly from the old habit of not wearing his glasses, and he seemed to be watching for some sign from among the markers that would be sure.

"Jolly? *Jolly.*"

"Hum?"

"Remember me?" The girl sat forward on his legs and leaned her head to one side in an attempt to bisect his line of vision.

"Sure, I remember you. You girl; me boy."

"Funny."

"This better?"

"Watch the tendrils," the girl giggled. "You shivering?"

"Well, it's cold, isn't it?"

Luke snorted once from the driver's side of the coupe and then resumed his half of the duet of smothered sounds, his patiently moving hands blocked as patiently by the girl.

The other nuzzled into the space between Jolly's shoulder and neck and fell to cracking her gum. "If you're cold it ain't my fault."

"Jesus," Jolly said in his teeth. He stretched his neck up and to the left in an attempt to escape the gum and the girl's mussed hair, which irritated the underside of his chin. The girl wasn't anybody special, just a friend of the girl with Luke, except younger, probably no more than fourteen. She wasn't even pretty, although if she learned to do something with her hair she'd be OK in another three or four years, what with those legs and a bosom that other girls her age blushed at and envied and which had already earned her mention by Ben Gusperson in the showers at school.

Nearly two hours ago Jolly had coaxed her to walk a ways down the grassy hill from the car, on the off side where there were yet no graves and from where she could see no headstone caught by the moon. She had hung back when they came to the three pines, and he had laughed and pulled at her hand and then hung his arm over her shoulder so she would not be afraid of the deep shadows, but she could not have said whether it was the dark she feared or the boy two years older who watched her bosom when he talked to her and now wanted her to go under the pine limbs with him.

"Jolly?" she had said as she pulled back a little, and the timid lift to the word was enough to tell him that she was afraid and the new brass of her in the daytime was there only because she was aware that the boys talked to her breasts that she couldn't do anything about and not to her. He had flattened the fluff of brown hair over her forehead and spoken gently, and she had, after all, gone under the pine limbs where the moon only streaked her skirt and legs and occasionally, when the wind dipped a limb, the blond head of the boy. She would have had less to fear and would have been warmer had she known what the boy knew. This was part of the game you played until you were sick in the bottom of your stomach. Sometimes you thought you'd win the game, but mostly you knew you wouldn't before it began.

Later they had climbed back up the silken-grassed slope to the car and he had slapped her behind to brush off the pine needles, he said, and she had laughed and didn't care now that nothing had really happened except that he knew that her breasts were not fake like that Ellen's who thought just because she was pretty and made high grades that she could get away with it.

"Luke? Hey!" he said.

He heard a muffled grunt, which would be Luke's response. The sound lifted at the end and implied a question.

"So let's cut, OK?"

Luke faced Jolly over the shoulder of his girl, who was also too unpretty to be of much interest in strong light and too young to be completely adaptable to the short seat of a coupe. In the moonlight Luke's face showed dark beneath an unkempt shock of straight black hair. Jolly knew without seeing that Luke wore his quizzical expression, one in fact that he was seldom without. Luke never took anyone at his word before first looking to see if he were serious.

"OK," he sighed. He disengaged himself enough to reach the minimum essentials for driving. "Don't sit on the gear-shift, honey. I can't compete with that."

The girl giggled. "Luke, you're awful!" She slapped his arm and chirruped.

Jolly wondered again how Luke got by with the things he said to girls and the things he purported to do. He wasn't particularly handsome or smart or athletic. In fact, he was somewhat on the plump side, which made his face babyish and uncomplicated, which may have been precisely where his charm lay. He never hurried, was seldom inspired by anything but his insatiable thoughts of sex, and was not truly upset by even that—not for long.

Nothing at all was said during the drive back into Cortez. Luke drove to the brown-haired girl's house first, shut off the motor, and prepared to re-engage the interest of his lady. Jolly walked with the girl to her door. She backed against the wall, and he kissed her, but his mouth was sore, and the game was over anyway. He smoothed the fluff of hair above her eyes and watched her arm cross automatically over her chest.

"Night, Jolly."

At the car he walked to the driver's side, got in and started the motor.

"That was a bit quick, friend," Luke grumped.

"Yeh. You guys about done in for the night?" There

was no answer but Jolly backed the car into the street and drove toward the second girl's house.

When Luke and the girl got out at her house, Jolly slid away from under the wheel and hunched into the opposite corner. He watched as the girl opened her door, reached in a hand to shut off the porch light, and as the moon settled slanting across the porch, he watched absently Luke's idea of an unforgettable parting.

"God, you sure take your time," he said as Luke flung himself back into his old Plymouth a long time later.

"Hell, man. You gotta work at these things *grad*ual."

"Yeh? Why?"

"No woman's gonna come across without you go nice and easy and cautious." Luke spoke slowly, dawdling over his words like a child with a treat.

Jolly hooted. "At your speed you'll be too old to do anything about it when one does come across."

"Huh. I notice you were doing pretty well there yourself for a while. What happened down in them trees?"

"She's too young and too scared. Besides, she's a pig."

Luke chuckled. "Well, like the man says, 'If they're old enough to bleed, they're—' "

"Yeh, I know. I know."

They weren't driving anywhere in particular, just around the streets, past the courthouse square opposite Cortez's infamous and continuous row of thirty-three taverns—one more than there were churches in town—that hung tenaciously to a time long past when the town was a famous cowboy stomping place, the revival of which occurred frantically for four days each year starting on the Fourth of July, down to the end of Montezuma Street, a U-turn in front of the colored Baptist church, back up the same street three miles to where it became a highway in front of the gaudily lighted Freddy's.

Luke swung the car precariously in among a double row of mongrel vehicles, each different, but all bearing the unmistakable identity of their alliance. A giant neon hamburger flashed mustard over the parked cars.

Inside the drive-in (no one wanted or expected outside service until summer) Jolly squinted his eyes against the light and smoke and wished he could squint his ears against the noise. The one big room was crowded, mostly with boys, although three or four late-hour girls huddled in the back booths drawing attention like manure draws horseflies, as Jolly remarked, mainly for the incredulous expression it brought to Luke's face.

They found room to sit at a booth already occupied by three boys in gold and purple athletic jackets who, because of their seniority, had grown lax in their training.

"You boys want burgers?" The worn waitress hazarded two more glasses of water among the debris on the table.

"Yeh. And a malt, baby," said Luke hungrily, although precisely the direction his hunger took was uncertain.

The waitress licked the tip of her pencil. Her eyes flicked tiredly over Luke's and came to rest on Jolly. "You?" she asked.

"Coffee and banana cream pie."

"We don't have no banana cream pie, and we never have had it and don't never expect to."

"Just coffee, then." Jolly watched her wag toward the kitchen, squeezing between the overflowing chairs in the aisles, lifting her arms and breasts, sucking in her stomach and hunching out her behind. Her blond hair struggled from side to side in asymmetrical rhythm with her hips. He watched until she leaned toward the kitchen serve-through to shriek her order.

When his eyes roved back to the table, Jolly found Ben Gusperson smirking. Guppy was a huge and pulpy eighteen whose fondest preoccupation, it was said, was divided between his naked image in the locker-room mirror and the telling of a bottomless supply of dirty jokes.

"You'd like some a that, huh?" grinned Guppy. "I can fix it for you, baby."

"Thanks. I can do without," said Jolly.

"Yeh. He's about the only guy I know can do without," said Luke.

But Guppy's mind had taken its tack, and now that he was launched on the topic he loved more than any, he leaned heavily over the table, drawing the two boys nearest him into secret allegiance by cupping a meaty hand over the backs of each of their necks. "Did I ever tell you guys about the time me and her was parked up at the lake?"

"No," said Luke.

"Yes," said Jolly.

Confused, Guppy looked from one to the other, searching for the truth, or at least for a signal to continue. "Well, do ya wanta hear about it, or not?"

"Yes," said Luke.

"No," said Jolly.

Jolly watched the color teeter on Guppy's face. Here it goes again, he thought. Someday, Jolly knew, he would push Guppy too far and would be the worse for it. One of Guppy's buddies, doubtless anxious to be relieved of the encircling hand, spoke judiciously. "Christ, Osment, do you *have* to blow smoke all over the place?"

Guppy seized the chance to direct any forthcoming ridicule away from himself. "Yeh, Osment, do ya hafta blow smoke all over me?"

"Yes," answered Jolly. "What am I supposed to do with it?"

"Ya got me. But if ya don't cut out that smoking you'll be in a helluva shape for track."

"I don't remember breaking any world's records last year."

"That's no shit," sniggered Guppy. "And you won't this year neither." He roared his great laughter and looked about for the appreciative response he expected. He got it. "An' besides. A guy as tall as you oughta be playin' basketball."

Jolly poured more sugar in his coffee, bent to meet the cup and tasted it before he answered. "Why?"

"Why!" exploded Guppy. "Well, just because anybody your height oughta play basketball. That's why, fer chrissake."

"I don't see much sense spending your life bouncing balls," said Jolly.

"Speaking of balls, Osment." No one laughed.

Jolly smiled slowly. "You've been peeking through the hole in the john again, Benjy."

Guppy grew livid. His great hands gripped the table and he looked like a swamp toad warming up to croak. Luke and the other boys appealed mutely to one another for a way to shift the topic before Guppy could get a grip on his temper and send it flying across the table in one fist. Before they could divert him, Guppy blurted, "You goddam—goddam—" The right word wouldn't come. "You'd rather play that goddam pi*ano* than a man's game!"

Jolly felt vaguely and carelessly that maybe this was it, finally. In a way, he would be just as glad to have it out with Guppy. Maybe they would leave each other alone after that. Yet he saw his chance to postpone the fight and took it. He leaned toward Guppy and grinned knowingly.

"What I do with my fingers and where I put them is my business," he said. He watched the effect register on Guppy's face. If there was an off-color connotation to be found in any remark, Guppy would find it; on this knowledge Jolly rested his defense.

It worked. Slowly a look of relief reached Guppy's face, and then his hands and shoulders. He looked to the others to see if the same thought had registered elsewhere. He threw back his head and laughed.

Luke leaned to Jolly. "Jesus, that was close. Let's shag before he changes his mind."

At the door of Freddy's, Jolly and Luke turned to listen to the howl of Guppy's laughter and watch the purple and gold giant beat the table and shake his head like a sorrel stallion in pasture. As they paid their bill, the same blond waitress touched Jolly's arm and leaned toward him over the counter.

"Aren't you Jamie's kid brother?"

"Yes. Yeh, I am." He watched the light seep up into her eyes, and although their gaze was distant and not on center with his, they held a soft-brownness not there before. "Why?" he said.

"No reason," she said. Then she added, "You ain't seen him lately, have you? No, I guess not." She laughed hard and short.

"No. Not for over two years," he said. He watched the light pale back from her eyes. "Look," he said and grinned, "can I help? Same family, you know."

The tired, vacant look returned and she straightened. Her eyes flicked down his length once, and she smiled on one side. "Same family, same equipment, eh?" She held out the change. "Don't answer that, kid. You'd just be braggin'. Here's your quarter."

She turned and her hair swung of its own weight over one shoulder. She walked to the swinging kitchen doors, this time with no wag, and through them. "Five minutes," she called to another girl, a pretty Mexican who was ladling soup from a huge polished pot into three bowls.

"I just checked, hon. He's okay."

The blond wiped the palms of her hands on her frilly apron and pushed open the door marked Women Employees Only. She pulled on a pale light above the sink and approached cautiously the cardboard box that lay on the floor next to the opposite wall. She knelt beside it. Before she tucked the blanket over the tiny fists, under the chin, she swept a long, loose strand of her hair back from her eyes. Tomorrow night, before she came to work, she would have to find a bigger box, maybe a nice wooden one, because he had about kicked his way out of this one already. She picked up his rubber dog from the floor where he had tossed it, and standing stiffly, she crossed to rinse it with hot water from the tap. Freddy Martinez had given her the toy for the baby when he was a year old, four months ago, after she had worked here for Freddy six months. He hadn't liked the idea of having the baby around the place at first, but he had finally agreed, only he had made her promise to be careful that they did not have a child because, as he pointed out, he had five already and it would be bad enough if his wife ever found out what kept him an hour later at night sometimes, and anyway, wasn't a favor deserving of a favor.

If she had had the strength left to hate, the blond girl would have hated Freddy Martinez, whose flesh was oily and soft and smelled always of cooking grease and French fried onions. But what had been hate for another had long since turned to something different; a kind of patience, perhaps, and a certain gladness that replaced hate when in the mornings she played with the robust boy whose black damp hair now curled over closed blue eyes.

"Where?" asked Luke as he flung the blue coupe squealing onto the highway.

"Home, Lucas, home," said Jolly.

"Already? You know you're not the greatest company in the world tonight, don't you? What's eatin' you anyway? You practically *threw* that big-tittied freshman outa the car tonight, and you damn near got yourself clobbered in there. And can't you open the wing if you're gonna blow more a that goddam smoke?"

"You through?"

"Yes."

"Well, number one; we got an English test in less than ten hours, including sleep."

Luke spoke one word, precisely enunciated.

"What did you say?"

"Skip it."

"Number two; if I'm lousy company it's probably because you pick the damn *mor*bidest places to park—like the graveyard, for crapssake."

"Cemetery."

Jolly rolled the back of his head on the back of the seat. "Okay, cemetery. Number three; nothing or nobody is eating me, but if you'd like to take a whirl . . . ?"

"Funny."

"Numbers four and five; I told you already she's a pig, and he's about the biggest horse's ass ever walked.

A regular animal farm I got on my hands. Number six; yes, I can open a window to let out the smoke, only make up your mind had you rather freeze to death or suffocate."

They drove along Whiskey Row in silence, both intent on seeing into as many bars as possible in an attempt to fathom the juke-lighted dimness that held unaccountable the mysteries of whiskey and pick-up girls and back-room gaming. Most of the places seemed empty, but from Friday night to Sunday night—or rather early Monday morning—they would seep their happy life, their smells, their guitar music, their destruction out onto Montezuma Street like sweat from giant pores. One loose-hipped woman clattered down the Row swinging her purse to some secret inside her home-parlored head, the iridescence of her skirt changing to match each flash of neon she passed. Luke slowed the car.

"Jeez," he said.

"Oh, for God's sake, Luke," said Jolly.

"Well, you never know. You gotta keep on the lookout."

"Yeh, you told me. Home."

Luke reluctantly shifted gears and turned the corner and nosed the car toward Jolly's side of town. "Rosy's got business tonight." Luke pointed toward a two-storied brick building, the bottom floor of which housed a colored tavern, the top floor (reached by a single steep flight of stairs behind a green door) of which housed Rosy and whatever charms she directed. "You got three dollars?"

"No, and neither do you and if you did you wouldn't have the nerve to spend it up there. Me neither."

Luke kept the motor running in front of Jolly's house. "See you tomorrow," he said, "and no kiddin', Joll, take it easy with Gusperson. Some day he's gonna chew you up."

"Will he eat me whole?"

Luke grinned. "Naw. He'll spit that part out."

Jolly stopped between the pines edging the path and viewed the little shingled house folded in among the trellised dead vines like an old barn owl impassively scanning the moonlight for prey, its glass eyes dimly reflecting the night. He walked to the back door and cautiously entered the kitchen as he always did, although knowing well his mother would be lying awake waiting for sound of him. He groped above his head for the string and pulled. Unshaded light sprang against the four walls as if it were desperate to escape the confinements of a room too small for a hundred watts.

"Is that you, Jolly?"

"Yes, Mom. It's me."

"What time is it?"

He knew she had already picked up, shook, and viewed her phosphorescent-faced clock. "It's late," he answered.

"Hum."

From her tight-lipped response Jolly knew she would have a word or two to say at breakfast in the morning, and she would roust him out of bed at least an hour early without having started the fire. Well, he could use the hour to study for the Great Hoary Father.

He rummaged in the refrigerator through habit more than hunger. He set out one of the quarts of milk and reached down a glass from an open shelf.

"They's cake," called his mother from her bed.

He smiled and rattled the cake cover so it would be known he appreciated the clue.

After he had placed the glass and plate in the sink, he entered the bathroom, which opened in an afterthought off the kitchen. He sat on the toilet and smoked a last cigarette after first opening a window. The room became cold immediately. He stretched over the tub to reach a towel, which he tucked around his bare thighs. But each time he lifted one hip to flick ashes into the toilet, the towel slipped away, exposing his flesh to the cold. Finally, he abandoned his legs to goose bumps and let the towel slide to the floor where it remained. Later, he examined his face in the mirror, memorizing the best way to hold a smile or the exact level at which his lids should rest in order to create the most awesome effect. The effect was short-lived, shattered by a frown at the sight of another new pimple. He searched a shelf above the basin until he found a small jar of medicated brown ointment, which he daubed over blemishes, real and imaginary.

Finding nothing else to do, Jolly faced the prospect of bed and the hour or more of sweet-sour restlessness he dreaded and looked forward to each night. He stepped from his clothes beside his cot (the same one he had slept in since he was eight) in the bedroom shared by his mother, only now the room was divided somewhat by a large pasteboard closet from Sears that housed his things, and he let himself noiselessly and naked into the bed, while from the other side of the partition his mother mentally shook her head, and she closed her ears against the sounds of this boy's night terror and ecstasy.

This boy—Jolly—wasn't like the other one. For that matter, as far as she could tell, he wasn't like anybody either on her side or his father's, not that she knew much about the man she had married late and lived with for a quarter of a century when he was home, and home had been a dozen places where he left her until he sent her money to move to another tiny, barren town where, he believed, his luck would turn. After twelve years of teaching in the same country school she and her six brothers and sisters had attended, passing twice each day over the same hickory-shaded foot bridge that led everywhere from her own father's farm, she had resigned herself to what her kindly older sisters called her "calling," watching silently as those sisters, and the younger one, and the boys each married and began to take hold in hilly Tennessee country.

For a year, between the ages of thirty-one and thirty-two, she watched the comings and goings of the blue-eyes-wild Jimmy Osment, who seemed to have swooped down from the north one day, from Indiana, some said. She watched the sawmill take shape from old ruins along Sandcastle Creek as she walked to and from the school. Mattawilde could not have said when the day came when she first paused in the obscurity of hickory shade to watch the brown, muscled back that seemed by nature to be turned. She could not have said whether she was shocked or intrigued by the tales that sprang up about his night work, which ranged, if the stories could be believed, not only throughout the whole length and width of their valley, but clear over the mountains into the next county, and farther. She did know personally one girl—only a slip of a girl, really, not more than seventeen or eighteen —who had taken that brown-edged white grin for more than it meant, and who had since moved away to live with an aunt for some months. Mattawilde could not have even said for sure the exact day when, after the mill was finished and operating, she had stopped beneath the limbs while a cold fall rain drizzled, and Jimmy Osment stepped into her path from the other side of a tree, grinning and cracking two hickory nuts together in his hand, sending the muscles of his arm pacing up to where the sleeve of his blue denim shirt was ripped off at the shoulder.

The first boy—Jamie—was like that. From the beginning he was lusty and belligerent and independent and blue-eyes-wild. With him Mattawilde knew what to expect—the unexpected—because Jamie was really Jimmy again. He seemed to have grown up before he was a child, and while they lived in the country (but now far to the west), before Jimmy died of a stupid, city-bred disease, Jamie at fifteen had already begun to range from their valley into the other valleys and then into town, sometimes not reappearing for three or four days, then to grin, and she couldn't be angry, and he would stay around home fighting with Jimmy, or leading his younger brother patiently over wide arcs in the hills and back home again for the days it took for his horse to rest and her to mend the rips and tears in his shirts.

Jamie never talked much. He didn't have to. She knew what was on his mind even when he said nothing. When his father died, Jamie showed the only sign of emotion he had ever shown to anyone, and that surprised her. He went on another year to finish high school in town, more, most believed, out of malice than from any desire to own a diploma. He came back once after that to the country place, and although he didn't say it, she knew as she mended his shirts that he was going—for good, probably. He did not say goodbye to her, but he did stop halfway down the lane, right before it bent out of sight, to pet Pekoe and lay his hand for a moment on the head of Jolly, who stood from his sticks-and-rocks ant corral to watch him turn the corner.

TWO

JAMIE OSMENT and Mandis Patterson were both awakened by the sun's first slant across their eyes. Both half turned where they slept and reached out a hand toward someone they expected to find. Neither found anyone. He blinked toward the sun, then hunkered himself and the wadded blanket over two feet until his head was again in the shadow of the shagged tamarisk. He turned his face into his arms and fought against the sun already mirroring across the river.

She bent the outstretched arm under herself and raised to peer into the crib. Her gaze, and then her smile, was met by the solemn blue eyes of the boy who had been watching her silently and wet for some minutes, his face tightly squeezed against two bars of the crib that hid enough of the sides of his face to make it look thin and 'possum-like. His white fists grasped two other bars. He was entirely still except for his bare legs, which hung on the outside of his crib and swung slowly out and back.

The woman seemed thinner and paler without make-up, without her nylon waitress uniform that at this moment hung miraculously perk where it had dripped itself dry during the night on its hanger crooked over the shower rod above the tub. In the green gown, its straps edged in frayed, stiff lace, her neck seemed long and the muscles of it tight beneath the long strands of vari-blond hair. But as she leaned from the bed to run her finger down the nose of the boy, her full body urged against the thin material of her gown.

As she changed the baby and then padded, her bare feet on bare linoleum floors, across the room to set him among the sun-strands, she talked to him—not as you would talk to a baby, but as if he were much older. He watched her as she moved, laughing afresh each time her voice began.

"You know who I thought—who I was dreaming about?" she said, and he laughed. "Yes, you know. But you can't know."

She took from the diminutive ice-box a bottle of milk, and a pan from the stove. "I think your eyes are getting bluer," she said. "Like his." The boy laughed but turned his startled gaze for a moment to a sparrow that flicked onto the window sill and off again to zip beyond his vision over the tar-topped roofs that squeezed like hunchbacked shoulders behind the apartment house.

"Sometimes I think you're a idiot. The way you laugh." She poured warm milk into the bowl of cereal and mixed it, then set it before the boy, between his knees. He smiled and dipped one hand into the bowl. "Ah, wait," she said. "I'll feed you." She wiped the hand on a red-edged cloth and sat before the boy to feed him.

"You know something? Someday. Someday," she said. "Stop that. You have to grow up, don't you?

Someday he'll see you, and you have to be big, don't you? You'll be big and black-haired and blue-eyed. Did you know that?"

The boy laughed and stretched out his oatmeal-slimed hand to touch the wet streaks on her face.

Jamie dug his face deeper into the blanket and flinched his shoulders to ward off a sticky ink-blue fly before he flung himself over angrily and sat up. He turned to stare at the bright water and the sand and yawned. He looked for his shirt. It lay a few feet away over the hood of his car—not a new car, but one that looked fast, lowered in the old style the way it was, with rear fender skirts that exposed only a shallow curve of white-walled tire sunk sadly into the scuffed sand. He focused on the shirt and willed it to come the ten feet to him. Deciding whether or not the fly and the cigarettes were reason enough to walk to the shirt occupied the time of another yawn. Then he saw his pants lying in a black crumple where they had fallen beside the fender. With almost meticulous concern he ran his hands along the outside of his thighs and looked to see what, if anything, remained on his person of his clothes. The revelation was enough to cause him to arise and grab up his clothes.

He buttoned his pants and then unbuttoned them again and stepped behind the tree in whose shadow he had earlier crept. Finding a tree was only part of country habit. Little obscurity this one offered on the long and wide stretch of sand dotted but sparsely with ugly tamarisks.

He shook the blanket violently to rid it of sand and began to fold it, making sure that the corners fitted precisely. From the rumpled sand he picked a barely-burned cigarette. Beside it, nearly buried, lay a black velvet hair ribbon that he turned over in his hand and then dropped again. He thought of the girl and laughed. She had been OK, but if she wanted to take off for town before it was really even light enough to see, that was also OK. She'd been willing enough to ride this far when he picked her up early the night before in the bus station at El Centro. "Which way you going?" she had asked in answer to his question. He had grinned and shrugged. "I don't care. That way, I guess," he said and nodded east. "All right," she said and swung her legs, knees together, around on the stool at the coffee counter.

Jamie threw the folded blanket onto the back seat of the car and grinned dimly to himself. They had spent the late hours of the night rolled together here in that blanket beside the river at Needles after she was practically hysterical from the cold, fast water and the wine and the sight of him standing white and dark above her.

She'd been OK, but she had wanted to talk, even after. She had said a lot of stupid things. Really funny, they were. And she had cried for a time. Finally he had told her if she didn't like his company just the way it was and the way it was going to be, she could get the hell out. "Out? Out!" she had screamed. "How much outer can you get?" She had untangled herself from the blanket and fished around in the car for her clothes. "*In*, that's what I want. Don't they have no hotels in this goddamn town?" She was really screwy from the wine and the drunk things she had said. He'd asked her why she didn't go see had they any hotels in this goddamn town, and she said that that was just exactly what she intended to do. He had watched her worm into her sweater in the pale glow of the car's dome light. She yanked her imitation leather suitcase from the back seat and faced him again. "Oh, don't you worry none about me," she said. "I can get work." He had laughed again and said he didn't doubt that. Only, he had added, if he was her he'd get himself checked by a doctor. That had stopped her in her high-heeled tracks. "What you mean?" she demanded. "You got something? What're you talking about?" He hadn't answered. "Jesus. I got pneumonia, probably, and sand and I don't know what all in it, and now you tell me. Jesus," she repeated. Jamie had lain on the blanket and listened to the angry scrunch of her shoes long after he couldn't see her at all in the swarthy dawn.

Jamie backed the car carefully through the sand up to the road that the conservation people had built along the beach. He listened to the sound of the engine for a time, then switched on the radio and slowly turned the dial until a clear station blared folk music.

He was only a hundred and fifty miles from home—or rather, from the house where his mother and Jolly now lived. He reckoned that he might as well push on. The postcard said he'd be there yesterday.

"His postcard said he'd be here yesterday. Now I'm worried." Mattawilde fussed at the kitchen stove. She snatched at the coffee pot when it began to spew over onto the electric burner.

"Two years and *now* you're worried?" Jolly dumped more sugar into the oatmeal. "I hate oatmeal," he said, adding butter and too much milk.

"Well, that's what you're getting. It's good for you."

"Yeh. Why's everything good for me that's either green or slimy? Or both. Like okra. Jeez."

"Hush up and eat or you'll be late. I hope he didn't wreck. He always did drive too fast, to my way of thinking. You want coffee? It isn't good for you," she said, but she set a cup by his plate.

"Don't worry, Mom. He'll be here. What're you so worked up about? He's been running loose since before I was born, it seems to me. This coffee tastes like the Mississippi."

"Well, don't drink it then. I got things on my mind this morning." She wiped her hands on her apron and took up her own cup.

Jolly added more sugar to the coffee. "I wish I had something on mine. I've got a test this morning on about a thousand years of American literature."

"You study? Never mind, Lord knows the answer to that."

"Well, if He knows the answers to that test, I could sure use—"

"Jolliff. Watch your mouth. And eat." She got up to run water in the dishpan that rocked slightly, its rim balanced on the edges of the sink.

"I already did."

"And speaking of books and things, I been taking notice of your reading matter lately."

"What reading matter? What's wrong with my reading matter?"

"That *King's Row* was out of the shelf. You didn't make a report on that, did you?"

"Sure I did. What's wrong with that?"

"I don't think you ought to be allowed to read that kind a book." Mattawilde flung soap powder into the dishwater. "Full a perverts, and I don't know what all. It's a regular come-off, that's what it is."

"Mother, I'm old enough to read what I please, it seems to me. It's just a story, after all."

"Well, you young people today read things I never read till I was grown and married. I don't know what's going to come of it."

"It's just been catching dust there for about fifty years. It's Jamie's book. If Jamie could read it, I don't see why I can't."

"Never you mind, young man. That's different."

"Yeh. What's so different about Jamie?" Jolly stood up from the table. "What's so—so different?" he finished weakly.

"Never mind, I said. You'll be late."

"Well, I just want you to know that if you think I learned anything I didn't already know, you're crazy—I mean, you're wrong. I could make you up a reading list that would—"

"That will do, Jolliff. You coming home for lunch?"

"No."

Mattawilde poured herself another cup of coffee and

sipped it, bent over the stove, delicately smacking her lips to taste the coffee. "See you eat something, hear?" She carried the cup to the table.

"You run along now, Jolly. I'm just going to sit here awhile and possess my soul."

THREE

LUKE's father, George Meaders, owned one of Cortez's two mortuaries. It occupied a towering remodeled home on the good side of town where the streets were shaded by rheumatic aspens of precisely the same age as the houses they shielded. It was called, simply, Meaders Mortuary, that being about the only difference between it and its longer-established rival, The Andersen Funeral Home, several blocks away and over one street.

Jolly Osment felt as nearly at home in Meaders Mortuary as did Luke, who lived upstairs with his father and mother. The two boys could have been found, had anyone reason to look, lurking in some dusky corner or peeping through the drapes from the music room during any funeral or vesper rosary. Before they were sixteen the two were allowed to help only to the extent of washing the great black cars, or spiriting the flowers out the back door after a funeral while the family and friends gathered at the front to await the emergence of the casket from the building—heaving them into the old pick-up truck and racing pell-mell to the cemetery in order to decorate the grave before the cortege arrived to find it miraculously bedecked in expensive sorrow.

Mr. Meaders would watch them dust out of the back lot until they disappeared down the alley, the sprays and baskets bouncing crazily about the bed of the truck. He never failed to shudder and touch his forehead in a sort of a posteriori blessing. Whether the flowers would arrive ahead of the procession, or at all, or whether—worst of all—they might designate the wrong grave, were some of the more serious worries George Meaders encountered in his business.

Luke would rage the old truck up and around the dirt hill that supported the Catholic school, down the other side onto the highway, across the bridge, the tracks, through Shaker Village, and through the iron gates into the cemetery, delighted to be driving the protesting vehicle as fast as it would go under what could be conceivably considered legal and emergency circumstances. The flowers always arrived on time and in passable condition; however, there was one occasion when the outcome was doubtful for a time. The day was overcast and chilly, and pools of water still stood on the pavement from a morning drizzle as Luke fishtailed onto the Shaker Village Road.

"Jeez, Luke. Won't this thing go any slower?"

"Sit tight, Joll. I think we're gonna do 'er in about seven minutes this trip."

"Great. And there'll be so many dead bodies all over the place they won't know who to bury."

Jolly looked through the back window as Luke vaulted the tracks just in time to see a large basket of flowers shoot perpendicularly off the truck bed. It tilted, suspended in air for a moment, then bounced onto the roadway on its one wicker foot and began spreading gladiolas in a shower of white on the pavement like some flower girl gone berserk at a wedding.

"Jesus Christ," said Jolly, "there goes 'Beloved Uncle.' "

Luke whirled to see what that meant, which was decidedly (as George Meaders concurred later) the wrong thing to do. When he looked over his left shoulder, Luke pulled the steering wheel in that direction. The pick-up began a slow, classical skid that transgressed a hundred and fifty feet of highway and eight feet of mud shoulder before coughing to rest against the bank, facing the direction whence it had come, leaving an elongated semi-circle of brightly-colored blooms and ribbons across the highway.

Jolly saw Luke's face pale beneath his dark skin. He watched open-mouthed as Luke tromped on the starter. From the old pick-up there came not even a final gasp.

"I'd say we've done it this time," said Jolly.

Cars began to line up along the highway in both directions. The people were reluctant to drive over the flowers that barred their way.

"Goddam. God*dam!* Shut up!" said Luke. "We gotta *do* somegoddamthing!"

At that time a lady left her car in the line and came puffing up, wide-eyed, to the pick-up. "Anybody hurt?" she trembled.

"Not nearly as much as they're going to be," muttered Jolly.

"Hey, lady, is that your car?" asked Luke, pointing to her big sedan.

"Why, yes. Yes," she said.

"Lady, we gotta use your car. Quick, open the trunk. Jolly, start gathering up these goddam—excuse me, lady—flowers."

In a moment the other bystanders who were close enough to see were swept up in the urgency of a situation they knew nothing about, and a maniacal harvest began on the Shaker Village Road. Bouquets and sprays were flung into the trunk, onto the back seat of the car, and hooked over the front fenders. At the very last an excited man came running from down the road with the traitorous white basket, cradling an armload of bespattered gladiolas. He heaved them onto the mass in the rear seat and stood back, panting and with frenzied eyes. All the while, the woman whose car had been usurped fluttered between the trunk and the front of the car. "Oh, my," she repeated.

"You ready, lady?" asked Luke.

"Ready? For what?"

"You ready to drive. You can drive, can't you?"

"Drive? Oh, my, yes. I can drive. Oh my, yes. Get in." She flung herself indelicately behind the wheel and roared the engine and began honking the horn incessantly.

"Jolly, you stay. Dad'll crap when he drives by here in the hearse and sees this mess. You signal him it's OK. OK?"

Jolly leaned against the pick-up and watched the crowd disperse. As they drove by slowly, they gaped at him and the truck and scratched their heads, or shook them more in disbelief of the role they had just played in some inexplicable game than at the catastrophe of the maimed truck.

Five minutes passed before the slow black cortege came into view over the railroad tracks. As the hearse drew abreast, with Luke's father driving, Jolly managed what he hoped was a reassuring smile and formed a circle with his thumb and forefinger to show that everything was under control. Luke's father touched his forehead in his secret sign and then faced the road ahead, ready to meet whatever further ruin the day might bring down upon his head.

Ordinarily, following a commonplace delivery, from the sanctity of the pick-up hidden in the pines, Luke and Jolly watched the dumb show enacted darkly time after time, the one nervously tapping his fingers on the wheel, anxious to be gone, the other silently intent, his eyes roving from the crowd to the grave to the barren area far beyond, to the mausoleum, and back again to the ceremony. Invariably, the shudder returned to quicken Jolly's spine, and invariably his mind turned back.

It had been seven years since his abortive child-visit to this cemetery, the only visit he had ever made in the private sense of the word. With Luke and the girls at night or with Luke and the flowers by day, going there was what might be called purposeful, not the same as private.

His private excursion to the cemetery had taken place long before Luke was known or girls were more than a bother, good, so far as anyone could tell, for throwing watermelon rinds at. Seven years ago, give a few months, when he was only nine, Jolly had formed the simple plot in his mind—a plot that he had dogged through to its end, even after the chances for its success had waned, because one does such things for one's father no matter how great a stranger that person is.

Jolly had wandered in from warming his plan in the morning air to ask his mother again. Maybe, he reasoned, if he asked her often enough, and directly, she would one day answer him directly before it was too late. He found her in the kitchen of the tiny house where he and she still lived, but now without Nell Ann, who that day sat cross-legged on a kitchen stool chattering and watching their mother work.

He had approached the kitchen door, silently forming the question he must have an answer to.

"Mama?" The word rose at the end like a question mark. "When's Memor'l Day coming?"

"Jolly-Bo, I told you before, it won't be long. Mercy, Nell Ann," she clucked to Jolly's sister, "I never *saw* a child so taken by Memorial Day."

"I know, Mother. He's more looking forward to that than his birthday. And them both not two weeks apart."

Jolly leaned, one bare foot atop the other, against the doorway of the kitchen. His attention alternated between listening to his mother and Nell Ann visit and the purply-white, fat turnip he had been frugally chewing since breakfast. He had learned some time long ago—or had been born with the knowledge—that if you used just your front teeth and scraped on a turnip or an apple it would last pretty nearly till the next meal. Only mostly his mother made him throw it away before he had finished, because he had used it for a number of other things, like ballast for his dump truck. It was a mystery to him why Mama wouldn't allow anybody to eat *any*thing that she figured to be dirty, even if it had only just been dropped accidentally on the floor and then picked up right quick.

Nell Ann uncrossed her plump silk legs. She said, "Can't you think of *nothing* you want for your birthday, Jolly?"

Jolly thought wildly and squinted at the turnip. He screwed up his eyes so they would know he was really trying. But he could not think of anything. "No'm," he said.

Mama detoured enough from her path between the four-legged electric stove and the kitchen table to rough her hand over Jolly's forehead and sweep back the sheaf of straw that hung there above his eyes. "Laws, I'll hafta cut your hair today if I can find time. Tomorra sure," she said and then passed on, her attention on the pot of turnips that sat among the faded yellow flowers of the oilcloth-topped table.

"You sure, Jolly?"

He watched the smoke from his sister's cigarette coil up until it spread out flat on the yellow ceiling and writhed among the electric cords that fed from the multiple outlets in the center—from which hung a bare bulb operated by a knotted string—and then looped away in several directions like black snakes after a winter's sleep.

The ceiling wasn't very high in this kitchen, not like in the big house out on the ranch where they had lived until last year. Living in Cortez had been exciting at first, especially in the winter when a person could slide so much better on the frozen cement hills. But now that summer was coming, Jolly missed the country where people didn't have to wear shoes every day if they didn't want to, and there weren't any sidewalks to burn your feet if you did go barefooted. There were a lot of other things he thought about some, too. He even missed the cows that chased him relentlessly. And the swamp and mulberries and Pekoe. He still didn't have it clear in his mind what they had done with Pekoe when they moved. Jolly imagined he was probably still sitting on the front porch steps out there, thumping his shaggy tail, with that sort of grin on his face just as he always had when Jolly came from school.

"Jolly, I'm talking to you!"

"Yes'm. I mean, no'm—I can't think of anything." He didn't like it when Nell Ann got up her bossy voice. He added, "I told you already."

"Mother, he's not even listening!"

"I am so! I want a racer bike with hand brakes and those skinny tires and a light and a horn and costs a hunnerd dollars."

"Joll," warned Mama, low. He knew he'd better be clearing out. As long as Mama said Jolly-Bo he had nothing to worry about. Sometimes still, in the evening when supper dishes were done and he sat by her rocker and read while she darned socks, her glasses riding low on her nose, she would call him Jolly-Bo-Bik'm-Bak'm. But the shorter the name became, the more serious. When she got all the way down to Joll then it was time to clear out before she started going the other way towards his full real name. Next it would be Jolliff or Jolliff Harrison, which was serious, but when she got to the whole thing—Jolliff Harrison Osment—it was too late.

"OK, I'm going outside."

"Where you going?"

"Nowhere. Just out front."

Mama's attention was already shoved between the boiling pot on the stove and its lid held above her head like one steaming cymbal as she bent to peer at the greens.

Jolly scuffed the distance down the dirt path between the two tired pines to the sidewalk. He sat on the curb with his feet drawn up close under him and studied the turnip. He wished somebody would explain, plainly, how long away Memorial Day was. Oh, he knew it was at the end of May, and that this was May. He could read that on the calendar. But that wasn't the same as somebody telling you, ex*plain*ing how long.

He scraped some more on the turnip and picked up a red ant between his thumb and finger, hard, as Jamie had shown him when they were still all together in the country. He dropped the ant onto an oily spot between his feet and bent over, his straw hair hanging down like a broom. Satisfied with the extent of its mutilation, he squashed it into the oil with his bare heel. He replaced his elbows on his knees and his chin in his hands with the turnip just resting against his left ear. He wondered for the thousandth time why, when you put something under your chin—like your hands or a table—your head moved up and down when you chewed.

Jolly had been pondering Memorial Day nearly ever since they had moved to town eight months before. He knew what the day was for; it was for memorying the dead. He was going to visit the graveyard this Memorial Day, alone. His mother had gone out there two or three times when she had some fitting roses or stock and someone to drive her. Jolly was waiting to make a special trip, and it had to be on Memorial Day. That was why it was so important that he know exactly the right day. If he wasn't careful, nobody would tell him when the day came and then the whole plan would be wrecked.

He knew the road to the graveyard, although he had been there but once, nearly two years ago. He would have to walk all the way, but hadn't he walked four miles every day since first grade? And more, if you counted playing. He pictured the graveyard in his mind and was glad he hadn't forgotten more; but then, he didn't remember it all either. The black cars he remembered, all the people he had never seen before, and more surprising, a lot right from the country where they had lived then. Flowers—those were what he had liked best—more flowers and bigger than Mama had ever had. Before the black cars there had been a man singing in the white dark house, a house here in Cortez somewhere, bigger than any he had ever seen before or since.

I come to the garden alone,
While the dew is still on the roses

The part he recalled hotly and never wanted to was when Mama and Nell Ann cried. And so had Jamie. Jolly cried, too, because Jamie had.

He skipped the remains of the turnip across the street and watched it bounce over the curb onto Mrs. Potter's lawn. She would complain to Mama again, probably. They would all be proud of him, he guessed, when they found out after Memorial Day what he had done. And Mama would write to tell Jamie, though Jamie wouldn't say anything about it when he answered.

Jolly hoped there would be some flowers to take.

There weren't any flowers except nasturtiums, anyway there weren't enough of any other kind in Mama's patches so she wouldn't miss them right away. But the day was perfect. The sun rose early and hot, bleaching the sky in a wide arc from the east. Jolly had arisen early and eaten his breakfast without complaint.

"Eat your breakfast, Jolly-Bo," his mother had admonished without glancing to see that he already had, "and then run along. I want you out from under my feet." She wanted Jolly out of her way, or anybody else for that matter, when she prepared to confront her monstrous green washer on Monday morning. She never entirely trusted the electric machine after nearly a half-century stooped over a washboard. To Jolly the Easy-Wash was definitely the most fascinating thing they owned, and he longed to work the gears and levers, but he could watch it thump and shudder only from the sanctity of the dining room.

This morning, Memorial Day, he was happy to be out from under foot, and he was happy in the knowledge that his mother's attentions would be completely absorbed, for the morning anyway. He stood by his cot in the corner of the bedroom and debated the question of shoes. The day was too nice for shoes, but the walk would be long and much of it on sidewalks. Besides, he decided, Memorial Day was sort of like Sunday in a way, so he guessed he had better wear his shoes.

It did not take long to reach the edge of town from Jolly's house. He followed his street down the hill where it ended, turned onto the street that crossed his and became, after a mile or so, Shaker Village Road. It would lead him eventually, he was sure, to his destination. Within a half-hour the sidewalk ended, and there were only a few houses now and then ensnared yellowly behind black grilled fences, decaying from a diabolical scheme to bring rococo and 19th Century Kansas City together in the West. Beyond the stone bridge that braved a dry ravine were the railroad tracks slicing bluely in the sun, and beyond those, the village.

Jolly walked off the pavement on the side of the road; his feet still felt more at home in the dirt. The bunch of yellow and orange nasturtiums hung limply from his off hand. When there were no cars in sight, he would lift them and inspect them critically. He knew flowers lasted longer if they were held upside down. Jamie had explained once that it was like the blood running to your head. You'd get dizzy, sure, but that was better than not having any blood in your head at all. It was another problem Jolly pondered once in a while, but this day he would take Jamie's word for it.

After he had walked about half the distance and was emerging from Shaker Village—not a village at all, but a cowboy hodgepodge of junk yards, second-hand stores, trailer camps and taverns—a car coming from behind slowed beside him. Nell Ann waved her cigaretted hand and called something Jolly could not hear plainly, then she and her gentleman friend sped away down the road and out of sight. Jolly paused a long moment beside the road. He hoped Nell Ann hadn't seen the nasturtiums. She would know right away he was up to something. Grown people, next to God, could always figure out what a person was *think*ing, even, if they'd a mind to.

Jolly saw the granite pillars of the gate long before he reached them. Walking along the high gray wall had depressed him—made him wonder if he should have come. Maybe only grown people could go into graveyards any time they wanted to. He wished he had asked about that, but then there had not been anyone he could have asked except his mother and she would have either murmured an indecisive answer or questioned him pointedly.

Once inside the black iron gates, swung open and locked to stone posts, Jolly hesitated. No one stood guard to send him away. He studied the beauty of the graveyard. Grass covered everything; the gently sloping hills—and the smaller hills—the mounds. Pines stalked the graveled walks that curved every which way among the white stones. Urns and sprays of fresh gladiolas and roses celebrated among the important-family plots nearest the main roadway. The effect was soothing and friendly.

Jolly was happy he had come.

He turned to the left along one of the wider paths. He was not surprised at all he saw; it was just as he remembered it to be. The nasturtiums, too, which seemed revived and relieved to be standing again, rollicked their heads as their bearer sunned his grin upon two men and a woman he met on the path. The three suffered the smile from a boy in checkered shirt and overalls without comment.

Near the center of the graveyard, upon the highest swelling of the ground among a circle of castellan pines, stood the arrogant and solemn mausoleum, the navel from which all the paths twisted on their daily rounds. Jolly stood for a long time and gazed at the mausoleum. It was as he remembered, only somewhat less awesome. Jamie had instructed him in the mysteries of the mausoleum. In there, Jolly had learned, they buried rich people right in the walls in drawers, and if anybody wanted to look at them, they had only to slide open the drawers.

"Mausoleum," Jolly said. It was a good word.

He turned his back to the granite building and faced the path he knew would take him, if he bore to the right some, to the grave he had come to visit. After five minutes of walking, he saw the grass less green. This, too, he remembered but had hoped was not so. The grass stopped completely and gave way to ever-lengthening horehound and to wild safflowers whose deranged yellow heads shook in disorder. He stopped to touch these plants that had been familiar to his every day when he had lived in Skull Valley, in the country. He was in no hurry to finish his journey, and, like in church, you weren't supposed to hurry too fast in graveyards, anyway, he reflected. He was a little sorry the weeds and wild plants were so tall because it made it hard to tell if you were walking on someone's grave.

There were no imposing white headstones in the section where Jolly walked; probably, he supposed, because it was a pretty new part. Instead, each grave was, or had been, designated with a small tin marker that framed, behind isinglass, a browned card that gave the vital statistics of the occupant beneath. Many of these had fallen over. Jolly stooped to straighten the ones nearest his path. He tried to read the names on some, but of those he could distinguish he did not know the people, and some were too faded to read at all.

He saw before him, near the path, two Mexican women standing so still they could have been taken for statues placed eccentrically to keep vigil over the grave by which they bowed, their hands clasped loosely in front, were it not for the capricious flutter of their black lace scarves in the breath of the noon day. Jolly hoped they would not pray too long, because a person cannot walk about when others are praying.

As he watched, each woman moved her hand vaguely about her face and chest, one more quickly than the other, and he saw that they had finished. When they lifted their heads Jolly saw they were old, like his mother; his throat welled up, and he knew he would be doing right to let them know that he understood and shared their troubles. He stepped to them with determination. The two pairs of mothery eyes watched him absently.

"I'm looking for my father's grave," he said clearly. "My father's buried here, too. I'm going to put these nasturtiums on his grave." He was proud that he would make them feel some better.

One of the old women began to whimper loudly into her shawl, and the two, arm in arm, bent back down the path and soon disappeared among the pines, leaving on the grave a Mason jar of red and blue wax roses.

"Well," Jolly thought, "I reckon I never said it right." He felt at last that he did not want to put off finding the grave any longer. He was in about the right place, he calculated, so he began his search in earnest, bent far over, straightening and reading the tin markers as he went.

He searched for an hour an ever-widening area before his tired back and the afternoon sun signaled it had been so long. He believed, stoically, that he would soon find the right tin poster, but as he rested his back against the hurt there, he saw stretch before him in every direction an endless maze of little markers slanting insanely among the weeds.

The boy paused for a second time before a mound that had no marker at all. He worried, briefly, that they might forget who was buried there and then how would anybody ever find out again?

He was glad when the first cloud slid over the west-slanting sun. He wondered vaguely what Mama would say because he had not been home for lunch. He fought against the panic and fury that arose in him because it was taking too long to find the grave, because maybe he hadn't remembered exactly as he believed.

"Ma'am?" he addressed another tired figure on the path, the first to whom he had spoken since his failure with the Mexican women. "Have you seen my daddy's grave? His name—" The woman passed on down the path, her head bending monotonously in order to better read the markers.

Jolly began his search all over again. Once he wiped the back of his hand across his eyes. "Darn it," he rebuked himself. He came to the unmarked grave again but hurried past, shaking his saffron head. When next he raised his eyes, he stood before the mausoleum once more. The façade with its low grilled doors, its windows high on either side, blocked his path stolidly and impersonally. He scowled and saw the polished monster blur and grin.

Again he turned his back to the giant tomb and took bearings on the graveyard. As he moved on the path he was not running exactly, but maybe fast walking was all right. When he found the nameless grave he dropped the wilted bouquet gently and without looking back scuffed purposefully away toward the gate and the road home.

As the broom-haired boy paused on the steps before his house, preparing to meet the rage of his mother, the sun dripped red over a swooping granite wall, the pines reached blackly against the sky, and orange and yellow blooms settled curling and scattered among the weeds.

That all happened half a life ago. Jolly, now nearly sixteen, yet remembered the day and the grave. He had never reapproached it beyond his mind, but he knew the direction it lay from wherever he and Luke obscured the pick-up—or at night, the car—among the pine groves. There would be a time, he vaguely knew, when he would face the unnamed grave's taunt, but not yet. Not yet. That is not the sort of failure one risks twice.

FOUR

AFTER Luke turned sixteen he spent the remaining two months until Jolly's birthday impatiently calculating how best to initiate Jolly to the mysteries of the preparation room. Of course, Luke had been allowed in there for several years, but George Meaders would not consent to his friends visiting farther back than the music room. After months of cajolery, he had promised Jolly the privilege of almost free rein—under Luke's tutelage—of the mortuary, a rein that had in actuality long been free, with the exception of the preparation room. Jolly himself, as his birthday approached, had oscillated between the pleasant prospect of driving legally, and the disquieting abeyance the thought of the preparation room brought to mind.

Luke did everything within the limits of an expansive imagination to create suspense as the day approached. "Wait'll you see the trocar in action," he taunted.

"What's a trocar?"

"Oh, you'll see."

"Thanks." Jolly waited, knowing Luke would expand the subject, given time.

"A trocar is this very long sharp instrument, see. It goes right about here." Luke poked a finger in the general area of Jolly's navel.

"Don't *jab*. What's it go there for?"

"How else you gonna get fluid in the cavity?"

"I give up."

"Smart-ass."

"Besides," said Jolly, "*I'm* not putting fluid in *any*-body's cavities."

"I'm going to ask Dad to let you do it, first thing. You'll probably get sicker'n hell, or something."

"You ever see me get sick? Except the time we drank that lousy pint of your dad's whiskey."

Luke smiled. "Yeh, as a matterafact. What about that movie, *Mom and Dad?* They practically had to carry you outa there on a stretcher."

"Well, that's different. I don't expect to be watching any goddam Caesarean births in the preparation room, for chrissake."

"You never know, you never know," intoned Luke mysteriously.

There was no business at the Meaders Mortuary on the day Jolly turned sixteen. Luke was in a funk about it and would have sulked at home had not Jolly insisted he drive his car to school so he could borrow it for his driver's examination after school. The thrill ordinarily expected with the acquisition of a Temporary Operator's License was to a great extent immolated to Luke's insistence that they remain that evening within range of the mortuary telephone.

"We going to sit here all night waiting for somebody to die?"

"Damn it." Luke cracked his knuckles. "Somebody's bound to die tonight, what with polio and all."

"You're crazy. Who's got polio?" Jolly shot another paper clip across the office with a rubber band.

"It's Friday night. Somebody'll get killed in a car wreck. Then you'll *really* see something. And stop flipping those goddam paper clips, can't you? You make me nervous."

Jolly shot two more clips at the wastebasket before he stopped and began searching the floor for them, collecting them in their blue box. "You're nervous! What about me? I'm the one who oughta be nervous. Trocars in your cavities. Jeez."

"Cavity, moron, not cavities. It goes in your stomach."

"Not my stomach, dad. And speaking of morons, what's *your* grade average at this second?"

"All right, all *right*," Luke waved his hands in exasperation. He walked the length of the room and back. "Your big brother get here? Jamie?"

"Yeh, he got here yesterday." Jolly picked up a crystal-ball paperweight and turned it over.

"Well?"

"Well what?" The little snow chips swirled and began to settle around the figure of an ice skater.

"Well, I don't know. What'd he have to say?"

Jolly swirled the snow again. "I haven't seen him."

"Whataya mean, you haven't seen him? Isn't he stayin' with you?"

"No."

"What's amatter with you now?"

He set the crystal snow storm down on the desk top. "Nothing. He just came in yesterday while I was at school, that's all. I don't know where he's staying. If he's staying at all. Probably with some goddam woman."

"Well, it looks like—," Luke began. "I mean, your own brother, for chrissake. What's he like, anyway?"

"Pale."

"What?"

"Mom says he's pale, and that's all the hell I know about it. So why don't you just shut up."

Luke flopped into a leather chair and picked up a magazine. "You're so gay and joyous you oughta be on the goddam stage."

"I'm sorry, Luke."

"Aw, screw yourself." Luke flicked the pages.

"Luke?" Jolly leaned back in the swivel chair at the desk and began shooting paper clips at the wastebasket again.

"Yeh?"

"You know what I'm going to do when I die?"

"Go to hell, for one thing," answered Luke morosely.

"Maybe, but anyway, I think I'll go to Andersen's to be embalmed." He leaped from his chair in time to dodge the ash tray flung across the room.

"All right, sourpuss. I'm going to play the organ."

"Whose organ?" Luke grinned.

"*Your* organ, friend."

As he passed into the chapel, Jolly ceased his laughing and walked slowly down the center aisle of the long room. He paused at the front and gazed into the casket of the tired-faced old lady who lay there and who had lain there for three days awaiting the convenience of her kin. Since no relatives had come forward, she would be buried by the county the following morning at the expense of one hundred and fifty dollars. Her head rested as if weightless on an over-sized satin pillow, her face composed above a pink frothy gown of the type furnished by funeral parlors and of a kind she probably never wore in life. Nestled among the ruffles at the bottom of the bodice were her hands, the left over the right, dark-veined and mottled. A single gold band shone thinly in the light of the chapel. Jolly bent over the diminutive form and curved a white lock of hair back into place above her forehead, and he turned her head a half inch more toward him, where it seemed to rest comfortably. He straightened and surveyed the cheap velour-covered casket whose only ornamentations were three stainless steel handles near his knees.

"I'll play you a funeral, old lady," he whispered.

He turned down the lights of the room until they glowed grayly from their indirect hiding places, then he drew back the drapes between the chapel and the music room.

With the switch on, the ancient black organ began its perpetual hum. He began playing from memory hymns of the type which he supposed all old ladies would like at their funeral.

Rock of Ages, cleft for me,
Let me hide myself in Thee;

Through the opening in the drapes, he watched the old lady's casket. He could just see her face above the edge. Her head, tilted toward him, seemed to take on an attitude of listening.

> When I draw this fleeting breath,
> When my eyes shall close in death,
> Rock of Ages, cleft for me,
> Let me hide myself in Thee.

He played "Nearer My God, to Thee" and "What a Friend We Have in Jesus," which were the only two others he could think of as being at all appropriate, before coming to the one he had reserved for last—one that he had never before played but knew well. He lowered the volume pedal and adjusted two of the dozen stops above the single keyboard. He played the song through once, experimentally. The second time, his eyes following his fingers, he began singing in a clear voice that had earned him the constant harassment of the church choir director.

> He speaks, and the sound of His voice
> Is so sweet the birds hush their singing,
> And the melody
> That He gave to me,
> Within my heart is ringing.

At the refrain he lifted his eyes but did not focus on the old lady's casket; rather, he watched a place on the wall of the chapel, near the ceiling, from whence glowed one of the hidden bulbs.

He finished the song as quietly as it had begun and reached to switch off the organ.

"Jolly."

"Luke! You scared the— you scared me."

"Jolly." Luke stood in the curtained doorway that led into the room where the families sat at funerals. "Thanks." He spoke strangely.

"For what, Luke?"

"That was a nice thing to do. You know she doesn't have no family or anything. That was a good thing to do."

Jolly swung his body around on the bench and faced Luke. He took off his glasses and rubbed them on his sleeve. "Don't be crazy, Luke. I was just practicing on this damn old organ."

No one died in Cortez on Friday night, May 17 of that year. At about the time that Luke, muttering over the inconsistencies of people's dying, let Jolly out at his house, Mandis Patterson opened the door of her apartment and felt her way to the dresser to turn on a dim light. She held the sleeping boy in one arm against her hip and talked to him.

"I wish you'd be awake," she said. "But it don't matter. He'll like you. When he knows."

She put the child in his crib and tucked his blue blanket carefully around him. "I wonder if he will come." She bent to kiss the child. "He'll like you. He's got to."

She hurried about the room straightening the cover on her bed, flinging stockings and her hair brush into a drawer of the peeled-veneer dresser. She unbuttoned the uniform and stepped out of it in the middle of the room and then hung it in the closet shielded by two short, flowered curtains hung from nails hammered into the top corners of the material. From a single plastic cleaner's bag she carefully removed the blue dress, and holding it by one shoulder she spread out the skirt with her other hand, then laid it across the bed.

She smiled at the blue dress. It was a good dress. It had cost twenty-five dollars on sale three years ago, and it had seen a lot happen to her. The first time she wore it was to her high-school graduation dance, and her corsage had been squashed and left a tiny stain on the shoulder that never would come out, but the big gold and rhinestone pin that looked something like a twelve-legged spider hid the spot. She wore it the first night she went out with Jamie, too, and she had to hide it in the back of her closet at home until she could mend it before her mother saw it. She had been wearing it the last night she saw Jamie. He told her then that he was leaving, and she had taken that pretty well and didn't know then that she was pregnant. When her father told her to leave home she had worn the dress so it wouldn't get crushed in the one suitcase he let her have. She hadn't worn it since.

But tonight was an occasion, wasn't it? He said, there in the restaurant—in Freddy's—he might come. He'd just walked in and ordered two hamburgers and coffee and she'd almost turned away from the counter without recognizing his face.

"What'll I do?" she asked the Mexican girl in the kitchen. "He's here! He's out there."

"Who's here? Who you talking about?"

"Sh." Mandis drew the girl to one side, away from

Freddy's vision as he sweated over the grill. "It's him. Jamie. The guy."

"Oh, my God," the Mexican girl breathed.

Well, she had faced him. She brought his two hamburgers and coffee and then stood there before him. He asked for ketchup. She brought it.

"Jamie?" she said, and for the first time he looked at her.

"Hello," he grinned, a tighter grin than it used to be.

"You don't remember me, do you," she said and untwined her hands from her apron.

"Well," Jamie hesitated. "I remember the face and the—" he waved his fork generally at her body. "Sure, I remember. You're—"

"Mandy," she said because she knew she couldn't stand it if he didn't know. "Mandy Patterson."

"Sure, Mandy. How've you been?"

"OK, Jamie. I'm OK." Freddy rang the pick-up bell angrily in the kitchen. "Just a minute," she said to Jamie. He stopped a hamburger halfway to his mouth to watch her move toward the kitchen.

He'd been willing enough to come up to the room after midnight when she got off. He'd looked a little surprised when she asked him, but he'd grinned and said sure, he'd probably be there. Well, she had another surprise for him. She wondered if he'd grin about that news.

She put on the blue dress. The zipper wouldn't close. She ought to have known that, after all this time. She pinned the dress closed. She sat before the dresser and combed her blond hair down long over her shoulders and inspected its roots. Then she wiped off the old makeup on a Kleenex, and, carefully bent toward the mirror, she worked on her eyebrows and lashes and her lips. She brushed off the shoulders of the dress with two or three impatient flicks of her hands. Standing back from the mirror she turned sideways to it, and placing her palms flat on her thighs, she tried to view all of her figure at once. She could not see it all here, but she had seen it enough in store windows she passed to know it was still all right. Except for a rounder stomach than before—and wasn't that to be expected—it was still OK—and bigger up above and that was good.

She moved the one chair closer to the window and sat gazing down into the dark street that ran by, three floors below, between the apartment building and the gray-stoned Baptist church that sulked across the way. Only now and then a car passed by up the hill away from town.

"He'll like you," she crooned to the sleeping child. "He's got to." She wondered what she was going to do when—if—he came. What could she do to make him stay this time? How, she wondered, do you make somebody feel the way you want them to? There wasn't any way that she knew of. She had tried holding out on them, and she had sure-god tried the other way. But one way didn't seem any more sure than the other. Maybe it was because she hadn't felt this way about any of the others. Maybe you both had to feel something at the same time. Not that there had been too many of them. After the baby—and Jamie was the first, no matter what they said about her in school—she had fooled around some with that big Gusperson kid and some of the other high-school boys, and there was that older guy, the bachelor, but he was scared. And then that bastard, Freddy. She hated Freddy, but then a person has to do something. If Jamie would just take her away from Freddy she'd be happy. She'd be satisfied.

When the knock sounded on the door she almost didn't hear it. She whirled to face the door and found she couldn't speak. The knock came again, more prolonged and a little louder.

"Come in," she said. She cleared her throat and repeated. "Come in." As the door opened her hands went to her hair lightly, and then she stood from the chair.

"Hi," he said and grinned. He closed the door.

"Hi, Jamie. Come in. Here, sit down. What's in the sack? Here, sit here." She had found her voice again, but now it was running away from her. "I put on my blue dress," she said.

Still grinning, he set the sack on the dresser and stepped nearer. "I see. You didn't have to do that for me. I didn't think we were going to church or anything."

She moved back a step, involuntarily. "Wait a minute, Jamie." She moved again so that his back was toward the crib. "Is that a bottle? Sit here." She turned the chair for him. "You want some ice?"

Jamie laughed. "OK. Have it your way." He sat on the chair and tilted it back against the side of the bed. He watched her open the icebox and take out a sack of store-bought cubes. "You're still OK, Mandy," he said.

"Sure. I'm just fine." She kept her back toward him and worked slowly over the ice and glasses.

"You're not kidding."

"You look different, Jamie. I mean, sort of white. Pale like." She turned with the glasses.

"Well, never mind that." He took the glass she extended. "Here, sit." He spread his legs some and dropped his hand on one knee.

She stepped back and drank from the glass. Might as well tell him now, she figured. Might as well see what's going to happen. She took another drink and moved past the foot of her bed and placed one hand on the crib. Jamie turned to watch her.

"Come here," she said.

"What the hell you got there?" He stood and peered over the bed. "Well, I'll be damned. That a baby?"

"Yes. Come here."

He stood beside her. "You got a husband around here someplace?"

She shook her head. "No," she said. "Do you like him?"

Jamie laughed shortly. "Well, yeh. I guess so. A kid's a kid, I guess." He drank the last of his drink. The ice cubes rattled in the glass. "Where'd you get him? Do you know—well, I mean, is he yours?"

"Yes," she said and faced him. "And yours."

"What?" He grinned. "What are you talking about? And I'm dry again."

She touched his arm. "Wait, Jamie. I'm saying this is our baby. Yours and mine."

He watched her face for a long moment while the

room whirled in front of her eyes. "What do you mean, it's ours, for chrissake? I haven't even seen you for years."

"Two years, Jamie. You left before I knew."

"How do you know it's mine?"

"I know what you're thinking. And a lot of it's true. But not till after, Jamie. Not till long after." She turned from his eyes toward the crib again. "He's yours, all right," she said. "Look at him, Jamie. Can't you see?"

He walked across the room. "No, I don't want to." His mind went back to that other baby, the one he himself had delivered. His stomach turned again. It always did. He wondered if it would ever not turn when he thought of that or saw pictures of new-born babies. Or even older babies. He sat down abruptly in the chair.

"Jamie? Listen, Jamie, I know we—"

"Shut up for a minute, can you? Just shut up for a minute." He bent forward with his hands on his face.

Mandy watched him from where she stood beside the crib. She held the railing tight with her hand to keep herself still. She stared at his back where the muscles were taut beneath the shirt, and at his head where the white, long fingertips were buried in his black hair. She knew that black hair, too; knew the coarse feel of it, had twisted it about her own fingers, and right now her fingers itched. God, she thought, what will he do? How else could I have said it? She could not know, of course, that it was less her news that troubled him, had only reminded him of another time and place.

"I'm going now," he said at last.

Be calm. Be reasonable. "Jamie, listen." She touched his shoulder. "You don't have to go." Maybe it would work again. After all, it had in the first place. "Look. You can stick around, can't you? We could—well," she laughed, "we could pick up where we stopped. Look, we'll forget about—"

Jamie placed both hands on her shoulders. "Stop, Mandy. It's not that. I'll come back tomorrow night."

"Will you, Jamie?"

"Yes," he grinned. "I promise. Only not now. Not right now."

She saw the gray door close from where she stood in the center of the room. She watched it as if it might open again and no longer be gray. At last she twisted her arms to the side to unfasten the pins in the blue dress.

FIVE

SOMEONE did die in Cortez on the next day, Saturday. A businessman, the nondescript man who sold typewriters at Case and Walker, and who plaited his long side hair over the top of his balding head. He left the store early in the afternoon, just to lie down awhile, he said, because his breath was short. Dozens, perhaps a hundred people passed him on the sidewalk as he walked the four blocks to his small house. Probably Jolly saw him pass from the store window at Penney's where he worked each Saturday and some afternoons helping the window decorator when he was not down in the basement licking price tags to stick on socks or shirts or underwear. At any rate, the man's breath grew shorter when he climbed the steps to his house, and it stopped altogether a few minutes after he had undressed and gone to bed.

When Jolly left the store at six o'clock, Luke was in front, leaning against the fender of the mortuary limousine. "Climb in, Jeeves," he called.

"Jeez, Luke. I can't drive a hearse."

"It idn't a hearse. And you might as well learn."

Jolly backed the long car out into the street. "Where?"

"The mortuary."

"The mortuary? Christ, I got to eat dinner sometime, you know." Jolly cautiously negotiated a corner that took them farther away from his own house. "What you grinning about?"

"We got one!" cried Luke exuberantly.

"One what? Talk sense."

"We got a case! A *body*. Dad promised to hold off till I can get you there and all. Hurry up, goddamit. You drive like an old lady or something."

"But I got to eat dinner," said Jolly as he turned the car onto the Meaders' tree-shaded street.

"You can eat later."

"I'll bet."

"You chickenin' out on me?"

"Hell, no, I'm not chickenin' out on anything. Here. You drive this train in the garage. I'll probably take off about six fenders."

George Meaders was waiting at his desk when Luke led Jolly in triumphantly. "Well, Jolly. Are you ready?" he asked.

Jolly answered with some difficulty. "Yes, sir."

"Let's get started then. This takes about an hour." He unlocked a drawer of his desk and deliberately set out a tall brown bottle of whiskey and a glass. He reflected a moment and then said, "You guys want a snort?"

Jolly turned to Luke for his clue. Luke beamed. "Yes, sir! Don't we, Jolly."

"Yeh. Yes, sir."

Luke's father reached into the drawer for two more shot glasses and ceremoniously filled the three. He handed one to each of the boys. "Now this isn't sippin' whiskey. It goes down in one bad gulp." He tipped back his head and drained the glass. Luke and Jolly did likewise. Tears sprang to Jolly's eyes almost instantly as the liquid seared all the way down to his stomach, but he was determined not to sputter and cough, whatever else he did.

"Steadies the hands," said George Meaders, heaving himself from his chair. "Come on, you two. We got an hour's work ahead of us."

The preparation room was disappointingly sterile, to Jolly's way of thinking. He forced himself to look about the white-painted room before focusing on the "case." One wall of the small room was lined with glass-fronted cabinets and held also a calendar depicting a big-breasted and denuded girl, her hands on her stiffly-locked knees, turned obliquely hind-wise to the camera, below whom ran the caption, "Our Supplies Are Better in the End," and below that in big letters, Adams-Addison Mortuary Supplies, Inc.

Against the opposite wall was set a large sink and a counter that held a contraption with hoses that resembled an office water cooler. The third wall was bare except for a chart such as Jolly had seen in biology class, tracing the veins and arteries in red and blue on a male figure, sans genitals. Near the fourth wall, by the door, lay a sheeted and lumpy figure. It lay on the wheeled stretcher from the hearse just as it had been placed sometime that afternoon.

George Meaders took off his coat and flung it onto a chair with his tie. He rolled back the sleeves of his wilted white shirt. Then he stepped over the stretcher and flipped back the sheet. "OK, you boys put him on the table," he said, indicating the high stainless steel operating table that could be pumped up or down like a barber's chair, or tilted like a see-saw.

"Why's he naked?" asked Jolly, stepping to the side of the stretcher opposite Luke. He hadn't expected the body to be naked. He hesitated before placing his hands under the white shoulders.

Luke grinned. "He died in his sleep this afternoon. Heart. I guess he slept in the raw. You better get over here on the same side as me. You have to lift a body both from the same side."

"Oh." Jolly stood next to Luke and together they slid their arms under the dead man's body and lifted. He was surprisingly heavy, and although not cold actually, his skin felt like candle wax; cool, but sort of soft and not unpleasant.

Jolly stood by and watched Luke and his father begin their work. Luke explained in an adulteration of technical language and his brand of slang each step of the procedure.

"He's making the incision there," indicating his father cutting a short lengthwise slit in the inside flesh of the thigh near the groin, "so he can get at a vein and a artery. You have to sever the vessels—one to let the blood out and the other to pump the embalming fluid in."

Luke's father clamped off the artery and vein on one side of the incision and attached a small yellow tube to one. The other end of the tube he placed in the sink. He then attached a similar tube, a red one, twining from the odd machine, to the other blood vessel.

"That one pumps in the fluid," explained Luke, "while the blood flows into the sink through the yellow one." He waited for his father's nod to switch on the machine. It hummed. The red tube undulated briefly as the pink liquid began flowing into the dead man's body.

"Is that all there is to it?" asked Jolly.

"Nearly," Luke winked. "Except the trocar. And he'll probably hafta make another incision under the arm since this guy's been dead quite a few hours. If he was fresh, one cut would do 'er."

Luke slipped a small rubber half-sphere under each eyelid of the body and closed the lids. "These here are rough, see? They keep the eyelids from coming open during a funeral and all, which shakes up the people considerable."

"God, I'll bet," Jolly concurred.

"Now he's gonna tie the mouth. Watch this."

Jolly found it hard to watch Luke's father wire the jaws shut from the inside, pull the wire tight, twist it and snip it off just outside the teeth. "When he seals the lips shut, you could never tell it," said Luke.

"Okay, Jolly," said Luke's father. "We're ready for the trocar." He handed the instrument to Jolly. It amounted to a quart jar of the pink fluid from the top of which projected a ten-inch, heavy needle that ended in a triangular-shaped point.

"Thanks, sir, but I'll just watch you this first time." Jolly extended the instrument to George Meaders gingerly.

"No, you go ahead. Just shove it in the cavity about here." He indicated a spot slightly above and to the side of the navel.

"You do it, Luke," Jolly pleaded.

"Go ahead, chicken. He can't feel it."

Luke took Jolly's hands and pointed the needle at the desired spot. *"Shove,"* he said. Jolly shoved. The needle pierced the skin and slipped into the body with surprising ease.

"Now what?"

"Fine," said George Meaders. "Now as the fluid drains into the cavity, just keep pointing the needle in different directions and at different depths until all the fluid's gone."

Jolly set his teeth and reminded himself that the man, indeed, could not feel the trocar probe his insides. The pink embalming fluid flowed out through the drill-sized needle slowly and evenly, disappearing somewhere under the flesh, filling the cavity. Each time the trocar bumped against or pierced an organ inside the dead man's body, Jolly could feel the marshy impact transmitted to his hands. He suppressed a hysterical giggle that rose unasked from the bottom of his stomach.

"What're you snorting about, horse's patootie?" asked Luke at his side.

"Nothing."

"Come on, what's so funny?"

The giggle burst from Jolly's lips despite his efforts to hold it. His shoulders trembled convulsively, and tears sprang down on his cheeks.

"Oh, Christ, there he goes again. You can pick the craziest times to get the gigglzes. You shoulda seen him at the movie the other night, Dad. The only person in the whole damn theater that laughed at the ending."

George Meaders looked up from his work. From above his steel-rimmed glasses he watched Jolly intently for a moment, then bent his attention to the suture he was tying. "Hum," he said.

"Had to wait about thirty hours for him to calm down before we could walk out in the goddam lobby," Luke went on. "All right, Osment, all *right*. Jeez, you give me the heebie-jeebies."

The liquid in the glass jar gurgled once and was gone.

"Remove it now," Luke's father said.

Jolly watched the needle slide out, clean. He had not expected it to be clean. The hole in the dead man's flesh remained open, a light wetness formed around its edge.

"Here," said Luke, extending a small plastic article to Jolly, "button him up."

Jolly held the item in his hand and turned it over. It resembled a button on one side, but on the other it rose to a tiny screw-shaped pyramid. He looked at Luke perplexed.

"Watch," said Luke. He took the button from Jolly, pushed it into the hole in the dead man's flesh, and screwed it twice. "Now he won't leak."

Jolly stared at the button incongruously attached to the pale flesh. He felt another giggle rise toward his throat but stalled it by looking away and speaking rapidly. "Now whataya do? When do you put the makeup on him? Do you put shorts or anything on him before you put on his regular clothes? When's the funeral?"

When Luke and his father had dressed the man in a white shirt and blue tie and a dark, pin-stripe suit, after transferring him to another table, George Meaders bent over the body once more and combed the gray hair smoothly back from his forehead. Suddenly Jolly allowed himself to recall that this was, or had been, a human being. The naked figure on whom they had just performed a miracle against decay became again a reposed, middle-aged man who had been—until this afternoon when he lay down for a nap—a busy, breathing, working man, someone's relative, someone's husband, someone's enemy; someone's father now at rest, ridiculously, on a bare wooden table in a suit without any back to it, furnished as part of the expense of being inalienably dead.

"Christ, I'm hungry. And Mom'll be madder'n hell. Drive me, Luke?"

SIX

JOLLY tossed his books onto the back shelf of the Blue Goose among the litter of red-penciled papers, backless textbooks, pencil stubs, athletic socks, one athletic supporter partially obscured inside a stiff, rolled towel, and two naked-breasted Hawaiian dolls whose grass hips wobbled on springs at the least provocation.

"Hey, horse patookus."

"Hey, Luke."

"You almost missed the train." The back tires spun in the gravel as Luke jostled into the line of cars waiting to cross the bridge.

"No feminine types, artist? You're losing your touch. More likely, you're touching too much."

"Yeh? What do squirrels gather in the fall?" The car squealed onto the pavement.

"Nuts. And keep your goddam hands to yourself."

"Look out. You damn near made me run over that old lady," Luke laughed.

"No points for old ladies."

Luke turned the car onto Montezuma Street and slowed for the cruise once around the courthouse plaza. "Well?" he asked. "Who'd you get?"

"For tomorrow night?"

"Yes. Some a your prizes or something, no doubt."

"Lucas, baby, you better get a good hold on it, because I really fixed us up this time."

"Who? Don't just set there, a-hole. Who'd you get?"

"For you, dad, I got Babe Wooten."

"No kidding? Wow!" Luke whistled once, long and shrill.

"And for me, Di Carson," Jolly said with more than a note of triumph.

"Now I know you're kidding."

"No crap. I really did. And you can pull in right there at Doogle's and buy me a big fat strawberry soda to prove your everlasting affection."

"Jeez, I'll buy ya two. No kidding? You wouldn't yank on an old buddy, would you?"

"Call 'em up, if you don't believe me."

The two boys pushed open the glass doors of Doogle's Center Drug and searched for vacant stools together. After they had given their order Luke whistled again. "I still don't believe it. Where'll we take 'em?" he asked.

"They want to go down to Skull Valley for the Saturday night dance. You want a cigarette?"

"No. Yes. This calls for a celebration."

"Look at the Baptist pillar, would you. Sin and shame."

Luke puffed at the cigarette awkwardly. "What do they want to go there for?"

"They've no doubt heard rumors that that's where the *big* boys go to play on a Saturday night."

"Yeh. Well, this boy's big enough to play. Babe

Wooten! God. Say, you've been to those dances before. What're they really like?"

"Jeez, I was about eight at the time."

"Eight! What the hell could you do at *eight,* for chrissake?"

"Very little except dance. As a matter of fact, at that age you went to them to dance. Real shit-kickin' music, too," Jolly winked.

"I bet." Luke blew smoke down a straw and watched it bubble out the top of his soda like a miniature strawberry volcano.

"Say, Joll," Luke whispered, "we better get some rubbers."

"Dreamer. Anyway, I have one."

"Where'd you get it?"

"Remember in that service station out by Freddy's? You got a package, too."

"Christ, that was six months ago. It won't be no good now, if it ever was."

"Why? I haven't used it—dammit."

Luke wagged his head in disgust. "Why, you can't keep 'em that long. They deter— tederio—"

"Deteriorate."

"Yeh. It'd be rotten by now. Why'd ya keep it so long?"

Jolly snorted. "What was I supposed to use it for, a goddam bal*loon?*"

Luke lowered his voice more. "Hey, Joll, we could buy some right here. Right over there. You just go put fifty cents on the counter and hold up two fingers. He'll know what you mean."

"Not me, dad. You ever done it?"

Luke bent his cigarette in an ash tray. "No," he said.

"Well, me neither. And I'm not about to. Couldn't you swipe some of your father's?"

"Hell, the last time I looked I couldn't find none. I don't think he uses them anymore or something."

"Do you reckon he's too old?" Jolly asked.

"I don't know. I wonder how old ya hafta be before you got to stop."

"What worries me is, how old do you hafta be to *start,* for chrissake."

"Tomorrow night could tell the tale, son." Luke swung off the stool. "Let's go."

They drove west across town, squinting against the four-thirty sun that cast long shadows from the trunks of the trees on the plaza, belying the heat. At the curb before Jolly's house Luke asked, "You seen your brother yet?"

Jolly lifted the door handle but did not open the door. "No," he said.

"Jesus Christ, he's been here a week. Or more. How come you haven't seen him?"

"Oh, I'll see him sometime, I guess." Jolly laughed, but shortly. "He seems to come calling when he knows I'm not here. Piss on him. I don't give a shit, any more."

Luke watched Jolly's face for a moment, then turned to face the windshield. "Yeh. Not much, you don't." Luke tapped the steering wheel with his fingers. "What the hell's the matter with him anyway? He must be as crazy as you—"

"Not a goddam thing's the matter with him."

"OK, OK. Well, patookus, you gettin' out?"

Jolly opened the door. "Yes."

"What do you wear to one a those dances, Joll?"

"If you don't want to look like a slicker, you'd better wear Levis. I told the girls we'd pick them up about nine. It takes about an hour to get there."

Luke grinned. "And about three to get back?"

"Depends on the circumcisions." Jolly shut the car door and ran up the path toward home as the Blue Goose's tires cried.

"Hi, Mom," Jolly said in passing on his way to the bedroom.

"Hi, Jolly-Bo. How was school?"

"OK."

His mother came to the door of the bedroom, a large wooden spoon in her hand. She pushed her old wobbly glasses down on her nose and peered over them. "You-all going out tonight after supper?" She pronounced the "r" like an "a."

"No. I don't think so." Jolly considered the advisability of telling her about his proposed plans for the following night. He decided for it. "We're going down to S.V. tomorrow night."

"What for?" She took off her glasses and wiped them carelessly on her gingham apron.

"Luke and I are taking some girls to the dance."

"The Skull Valley dance?"

Jolly heard the edge tighten about her lips. "You-all got no business at that dance."

"Aw, Mom. I went when I was six, for chrissake. Excuse me."

"You *better* watch your language, young man. It's a crying shame the way you talk. Hang that shirt up. And that was different. You didn't know anything that was going on when you were six. Anyway, I think you were at least eight before I let you go."

"OK, Mom, OK. You gonna stand right there? I'm changing clothes, you know."

She didn't leave, but she turned her head to face the other room. "Who are the girls?"

"Just some girls at school. You don't know them."

"Do they go to our church?"

"No. I think they're Methodists, or Episcopalians, or something."

She turned her head back toward him and stepped closer. "You been smoking again, haven't you. Don't tell me different. I can smell you from here to kingdom come. It's a crying shame. Smoking and dancing and staying out half the night and I don't know what all. Lord have *mercy,* I wish your father was here. He'd put a stop to it. Put on some shoes. I want you to run to the store for me 'fore supper."

"I don't need shoes on to go to the store," Jolly said, happy to change a subject he wished he had never mentioned. "It's only two blocks. What do you want?"

"Here's a little list. And don't buy those vegetables 'less they're good an' fresh. Now run along," she said, moving back into her kitchen, wooden spoon poised.

Jolly found a pine cone in the path leading from his

house. He kicked it with his bare toes twice before it bounced away into a shrub. He walked in the dirt easement between the sidewalk and the street down to Mrs. Adlow's house. There he stepped up on her low brick wall and with exaggerated waving of arms balanced himself to the corner of the first block.

"Off that wall, young man," called Mrs. Adlow from her flower bed at the angle of the wall.

Jolly stood atop the wall and gazed down on her. "Your petunias are beautiful this year, Mrs. Adlow."

A smile overtook the unnatural frown on her face. "Why, thank you, Jolly. Do you really think so? I was afraid they weren't going to do so good this year. They got a late start. Mr. Adlow said they'd never amount to a thing, but I told him that if anybody could make 'em grow, I could, so I just got out here and—"

Jolly jumped off the wall and continued his own thoughts, leaving Mrs. Adlow's ruffled petunias to hear hers.

His thoughts returned to Di Carson, and as he reviewed her known file, he wondered again why, when you diagrammed complex sentences and parenthesized the American Revolution with dates, you used your head, but when you thought of girls, and boys and girls, you used your stomach. Maybe after tomorrow night... Well, if anybody would, Di would. Everybody said so. Weren't she and Babe Wooten known in the locker room as the dirty duo? He swung precariously from a too-young aspen limb that bent out over the sidewalk. Would he know what to do if she would, he wondered. Everybody said you would know when the time came, never fear. He had asked Jamie about that, too, two years ago when he had come home for three days. Yes, Jamie had agreed, you'd know when the time was right, and he'd grinned when Jolly admitted, at fourteen, that the nearest thing he'd ever done to or had done by a girl hearkened back to before Jamie had left home in Skull Valley when he and Jolly came upon Francee Epum in the swamp, and Jamie had made Francee let Jolly stay for a while until he had a chance to see her undressed, and she had made Jolly drop his pants, too, as payment. She had laughed and measured the difference between the little brother and the big one before Jamie had sent him on home with Pekoe.

And Guppy, who was too simple to lie, just three weeks ago told Jolly and Luke and a half-dozen others in the gymnasium basement how he had lured Di, without much trouble, down there during a school dance and showed them the bench that ran before his locker where she had lain and how much trouble it was, the two of them trying not to teeter off the narrow bench and how they took a shower together afterwards where things got out of hand again. Jolly believed him because when he had finished his eyes were vacant, and he walked to the other end of the locker room and shut himself in the coach's john, the one with the metal door; that and a certain reverent tone of voice like a country preacher revealing for the first time the wonders of Sodom and Gomorrah to a barefooted, toe-twisting shock of Sunday angels.

SEVEN

AS THE long black car dipped down the last hill its headlights struck the shallow water of Hassayampa Creek, which signaled the beginning of the valley proper. The four of them were riding in the front seat of the mortuary limousine. Behind them, like a different room, the interior of the over-sized car stretched away solemnly.

For the last few minutes Jolly had not spoken. With his forehead pressed against the window glass he watched for signs of anything familiar along the roadside in the new night. He wished it were daylight to better see those things that he had not seen once in eight years.

The first recognizable object was the silhouette of the ruined adobe wall, momentarily visible against the skyline, which surrounded twenty low heaps of stones, purportedly the time-forgotten burial grounds of some small Indian band whose numbers had been further diminished at this spot by an encounter with white men, or perhaps another, hostile, Indian tribe. Jolly opened his mouth to speak, to explain the interest of the adobe wall, but no one else had seen it, evidently. He said nothing and saw nothing else within memory, except the two-lane dirt road ducking and hiding from the car's headlights, until they came to the white creek.

"What the hell's water doing in the middle of the road?" asked Luke, stepping too hard on the brakes. The car slid down to the edge of the water where it stopped while the dust rolled over the hood and pranced in the beams.

"Not deep," said Jolly. "Go on across." He watched the water separate to the side of the car and ripple in dwarf rage. If you drank from the Hassayampa, it was said, you'd never again speak the truth.

Immediately beyond, Jolly saw the great trunks of the cottonwoods standing crooked and pale around what had been a favorite church picnic grounds, and he recalled, incongruously, the embarrassment Bethamae Epum had caused him by complaining shrilly to their Sunday School teacher that he had purposely hiked up her dress.

"You guys bring any more beer?" Babe Wooten was asking.

The narrow road that led into the hills and eventually to the Cranshaver's where no one had ever trespassed and where, it was said, their idiot boy was chained in a lean-to and ate from the same dish with the dogs.

> Oh I had lotsa trouble makin' Mary,
> Mary's ma and paw don't care for me,

Luke sang.

The lake, how little it looked now lying flat and undisturbed by moonlight, where they—Jolly and Jamie—had pulled the still gasping body of Mickey Fernandez out by his ankles one afternoon and watched, frenzied, as his eyes rolled back under the curls on his forehead, and he died in the wet reeds at their feet.

So just to save a fight,
And make everything all right,
I'll meet my Mary by the zoo, you see.

The hill behind Old Lady Decker's cheerless hermitage, eroded, its few trees growing at angles from the clay, where each summer the torrential rains disemboweled another of her ancestors to send his bones and decayed cottonwood coffin slithering down into the road where they remained except for what the dogs scavenged until someone called for a county official who shoveled them onto his truck and drove away, where, no one asked.

On Monday I'll have Mary by the camels,
That's the place that Mary oughta be,

The lame fieldstone house where the two simple sisters, Clara and Eva, had lived alone since long before their memory when they were not out foraging in someone's apple orchard or melon field and who bought a new gas stove when there had never been electricity to Skull Valley much less gas and who walked to their nearest neighbors every day for assistance in lighting the stove.

Tuesday by the bears,
Wednesday by the hares,

The general store shrinking with age nevertheless as indominable as its mistress who operated it before, during, and after four husbands in succession, the last of whom died of pneumonia from lying on his back in the rain to tinker with the undersides of his jalopy, and which housed a cache of out-priced candy and soda pop—fascinating to the eyes of a child who never tasted of either except at Christmas—as well as a minute post office for persons who could afford a dollar a month for the privilege of twisting a brass combination lock or who otherwise had to ask for their mail at the barred window providing the proprietess was not busy in another part of the store.

Thursday by the deer, my dear, you see.

The stone bridge over Kirkland Creek spanning an ordinarily dry bed of sand that two or three times a year raged and foamed about the ankles of a small boy who had to cross it two miles farther down on his way home from school in the company of his older brother, who scoffed at the treachery of the water until one spring one of his own friends was surprised while in the middle of the creek bed by the four-foot tumble of muddy water roaring down upon him from the mountains and whose arms flung over his head were little defense against the maelstrom that carried his body seventeen miles and three days and left it like a hapless yearling butchered in a barbed wire cage beside the creek.

On Friday I'll have Mary by the monkies,
Swingin' on her little rings of brass,

The little green-roofed cabin, now tilting precariously toward the creek bed where clubfooted Harry

Band—called Bandy by the adults and Harry the Happy Homo by Jamie and the big boys—had lived for ten years content to do part-time work in the general store for his meals and lodging until he was found one morning in his cabin unclothed, his head bashed in with his own specially-built shoe by a passing hobo, some thought, although a coffee can of small bills and change sat undisturbed on a bedside table and it could have been any one of several young men to whom Bandy offered a drink and affection.

On Saturday I'll have Mary by the donkies,
That's the time that I'll have
Mary by the ass!

The white stucco school—its two long rooms divided by a central hall that ended where the bell rope hung down awaiting as reward to a well-behaved boy or girl heavy enough to turn the great rusted bell—whose wrought iron and wooden-topped desks held the ink and knife cuts of a thousand secrets and spring agonies—whose thin-worn chalkboards had felt the thrill of words and the terror of numbers transmitted to them from countless sweaty hands—behind which stood the hedge now much taller through which Jolly and Rachet had watched their older brothers engage Anna Lou Inkner in sexual intercourse after school one day and which they interpreted conjointly as a pretty silly way to take a leak—between a girl's legs.

"Where *is* this place, Jolly?" asked Di Carson. She leaned forward to tap her cigarette on the edge of the ash tray. "You're not exactly a terrific conversationalist, you know." Jolly watched the back of her neck and bare shoulders ripple in the muted reflection from the car's lights. Her hair was caught with a green ribbon and hung white and long, straight down between her shoulder blades. He reached one hand forward and pressed the tail of hair against her flesh. Her head lifted, and beneath his hand he felt her body tense. She pushed slowly until his hand lay between her back and the seat. She turned toward him, eyebrows lifted, her lids nearly closed, a faint dimple playing at one corner of her lips whose heavy paint made them black in the dim light. His hand slid across her back as she twisted, and entered, as if by accident, between her dress and her skin under her arm. Because the soft lump of flesh startled him, he would have withdrawn his hand had she not stayed it with one of her own. She had begun to mutter something when his mouth closed the last inch gap. His other hand covered hers as it moved to his leg.

"This the place, Joll?" Luke asked, imperviously.

Jolly withdrew his hand. "Yes," he said. "There. You turn in down there at the gate."

Luke eased the heavy car through the gate, over the cattle-guard, and in among perhaps fifty cars parked disorderedly before a long and low building—a building known as the Community Hall—that would reverberate to the booted feet of a hundred latter-day cowboys and farmers and their moccasin-footed women until perhaps three or four o'clock in the morning, at which time Ben the janitor would begin his weekly transformatory ablutions that caused Community Hall to become Community Church in which many of these same men and women would gather again at ten o'clock on Sunday morning.

Bright yellow light streamed from two doors propped open to catch the breeze. From across the parking lot, before the music could actually be heard, could be felt an indefinable vibration of thumping instruments and pounding feet. Among the cars in the lot were three or four small groups of people, mostly men, gathered in starlit communion with a bottle of whiskey. By midnight most of the bottles would be empty and only couples would be seen in or among the cars. Those young men left without female consort by that time would have already gathered once or twice behind the hall to watch two of their friends roll furiously and silently in the dust like hot-blooded bulls testing their first year's horns.

At the door of the hall Luke and Jolly paid a dollar and a half each for the tickets to a white-haired and bosomy lady who stamped the backs of their left hands with a purple three-leaf clover.

"God, look at the hicks," said Babe Wooten, squinting into the convolution of children and adults.

"I'm looking, I'm *look*ing!" said Di Carson. The others turned to her, sensing the thrill in her voice, and followed her impudent gaze.

Against the near wall coursed the stag line, which moved with one Stetsoned head, one pair of insolent eyes, watching its prey enter the door, calculating the possibilities of intrusion from the gait of the girls and the size of their escorts. The brim of its tan hat curled convulsively to either side of a point set so low above the eyes that its head tilted backward perpetually in order for the eyes to see at all. Turned high among curls on the back of the neck was the collar of a custom-tailored, long-sleeved and flowered shirt, so tight that the nipple of the left breast pointed under the double thickness of a pocket, the right breast bared—except for black damp hair—weighted open by a row of pearl snaps repeated on the long, closed cuffs. The thumbs hooked into back pockets of Levis carefully shrunk and stitched so that not an excess wrinkle could appear anywhere except across the groin to accentuate genitals held high and forward. Hidden beneath the Levis—but for the toe and high riding heels—were the boots, the left crossed over the instep of the right. The only portion of the body to touch the wall was a point high between the shoulders in order that the delicate hips remained thrust forward.

Jolly felt the color rise to his face and heard Di stifle a low moan that seemed not to issue from her lips but from a spot farther down, below the surface. Jolly glanced at his own clothes and damned himself. He too wore Levis and a pearl-snapped shirt, but the effect was casual, unstudied, wrong.

"Let's dance." He pulled her to him roughly. Whirling her into the melee, he made his way as quickly as possible, despite kicks and elbows, across the dance floor, near the stage where the three-piece band played.

"They make a hell of a racket, don't they," he said to Di in a desperate attempt to divert her attention. "That's Old Lady and Mr. Coon playing the guitar and fiddle. That's Mrs. Decker beating the piano. She only comes out of her hole on Saturday nights to play those same three chords over and over for six or seven hours.'' He was breathless, and he felt the beer they had drunk in the car begin to fog, and he was afraid he would soon babble.

''The Old Coons must be about a hundred. But they still keep playing every week. I guess. She calls the square dances, too. They'll do some square dancing tonight, I imagine. You ever square-danced? He drinks about a barrel every night. When I was a little boy he used to tell me that if I'd do the church-going for him he'd do the whiskey-drinking for me. Ha, ha. I wonder if he—''

''Take it easy, stud.'' Di lifted her lips and breathed on his neck. ''Take it easy.'' She stretched back her neck and studied his face curiously. ''The beer gettin' you? I never heard you talk so much.''

He pulled her head into his shoulder and raised his right hand until it spread over the bare skin of her back. ''No. There's nothing the matter with me.'' Her skin was damp and cool to touch, but it seemed to have a second layer beneath the cool one that was warm. He moved his hand down to her waist where there was cloth again. Beneath the pressure of his fingers her hips moved forward to meet his. Gradually his steps slowed until they were standing nearly still. Around them couples whirled; the bright full skirts of the women swept round and round, punctuated by the long, blue, stamping legs of the men. To Jolly, as his head bent beside Di's so that his chin just touched her shoulder, close to her neck, there seemed to be no bodies above the whirling skirts and legs. His eyes fixed as if stunned, he saw the colors flash, and he shared, rather than heard, the beat of the music and the steady delicious rhythm of the dancers. Nearly motionless, Jolly felt insanely that all the heat of the crowded room had been gathered up into that one spot between him and Di where her hips moved to return to him each thrust of his own. When the music stopped, he believed for a moment that he could not remember how to step back, how to separate himself from her. His shirt stuck to his chest where he had pressed himself too hard against her.

Di brushed the hair back on her temples. The dimple skirted one corner of her lips again. Curious, her eyes watched Jolly's. He followed a drop of perspiration as it slipped down her neck, hesitated, then wriggled like some giant amoeba down the cleavage of her breasts. He wanted to put his thumb there to stop it before it ran from sight.

"Hey," she said. Her hand covered his, but she did not remove it right away. She laughed slowly and low. "I see why the guys call you Fingers."

"They got any Cokes or anything to drink here?" she asked, looking vaguely about the room.

"Yeh. Over there." He indicated a wide serve-through opening from the kitchen. "They've probably got Cokes and all." She began to lead him across the floor, but he tugged back on her hand.

"Di," he said. "Wait. Wait a minute.'

She turned to face him. "What's the matter with your voice?" she asked.

"Nothing," he said. "Let's go outside awhile."

"Outside?"

"Yes. To the car. You want to go to the car awhile?" He began to pull her hand toward him.

Di did not move. She plucked at Jolly's arm with her other hand and said "Jolly?" in an incredible, little voice. He saw that her eyes had grown wide and stared past him, over his shoulder.

Jolly turned. There behind him stood a young man who had been watching the back of his neck, evidently, but who now shifted his eyes darkly to meet Jolly's. Held slightly before him in one hand, the blade just resting on the other palm, was a knife glinting bluely against his flowered shirt.

Jolly's gaze dropped to the knife and then back quickly to the lips curled over a hand-rolled cigarette, then on to the man's eyes, one of which squinted against the smoke.

"Bill!" Jolly exploded. "Bill Kemp!"

"H'lo, you little bastard. Thought it uz you." The man's lips smiled on the side opposite the cigarette. "I'm still gonna cut off yer goddam ears." He brandished the knife.

Jolly laughed. "You scared the crap outta me, Bill. What are you still doing around here, anyway?"

"Waitin' to cut off yer goddam ears." The young man's eyes flicked sideways to Di, then slid down her and back to Jolly. "Er maybe you ready to have somethin' else cut off by now.'' Jolly could smell the whiskey on his breath.

''Bill, this is Diane Carson. Bill's been threatening to cut off my ears for the last ten years since I surprised him and a heifer in his dad's barn one day.''

''Never mind, Osment, never you mind,'' spoke Bill Kemp quietly. His eyes traced Di's body insolently. ''I tell ya what, Osment, you little sonuvabitch. I won't never cut off yer goddam ears ner nothin' else if ya let me have at it with yer lady this dance.'' He smiled at Jolly. ''Course it won't make no difference if ya let me 'r not, ya know.''

Jolly reached for Di's hand again. ''How about a little later, Bill. Di and I were just going out for a—for a while. A beer,'' he stammered.

Bill Kemp did not say anything. Neither did Di. They only watched each other.

''Come on, Di,'' Jolly said. He felt her slipping away even before her hand did. ''We could just have a beer.'' He knew the back of his neck was turning red. ''Dammit, Bill,'' he said, ''Goddamit!''

Bill's eyes never left Di's, but his right arm swung up a little, an almost imperceptible bit, and from his hand the knife blade caught dull light and winked.

Jolly felt Di's hand pull from his. She moved into Bill's arms as if she had danced with him all her life. Or had been practicing for the occasion. Jolly walked to the wall and squatted there and lit a cigarette. He saw Di's green skirt disappear into the crowd beside Bill's long, blue-fitted legs.

Bill Kemp must be about twenty-two or twenty-three,

Jolly figured. It was a wonder he remained in Skull Valley, but then people had said Bill Kemp would never amount to anything—the Kemps never did. After the day Jolly came upon Bill in the act of attempted sodomy with the heifer, they became friends of a sort —at least Bill took time to pull out his knife and joke with Jolly at the Saturday night dances—and that same afternoon, Bill, at that time twice his age, introduced Jolly to the mystery of masturbation, an act beyond the power of the seven-year-old, but it provided information that, stored away, was of use five years later.

A pair of pillar legs hove into Jolly line of vision and stopped, thigh-level with his face. Before looking upward his eyes were drawn down the meshed legs to where they overhung white comfort oxfords. "Mrs. Arney!" he said, before seeing her face. He dropped his cigarette on the floor and stood.

"Jolly Osment, I declare. I thought 'twas you a-settin' there like a blessed injun." Mrs. Arney's wide face broke in all directions.

"Hello, Mrs. Arney. Yes, it's me."

"Well, I declare. How you've growed! Last time I seen you you weren't taller'n a minute." Her body shook in gargantuan merriment.

"Yes, ma'am. I guess I have grown some."

"Still a-goin' to Sunday School?" Mrs. Arney had commandeered all the boys and girls of the valley above the age of four for twenty-five years. "Ours is still a-goin' strong." She raced up and down the valley every Sunday morning in her ancient school bus gathering in her flock.

"Yes'm. I still go some—to church." Jolly glanced beyond her at the whirling colors.

Her bosom began shaking before the laugh sounded in her throat. "That's a blessin' truly. Like I was sayin' to the Lord the other night—how's Mattawilde?"

"What? Oh, Mother. She's fine, thanks. She—"

"Like I was sayin' to the Lord the other night, maybe He got caught up on His rest on Sundays, but I swan if some a His shepherds—I like to think of myself as a shepherd, which ain't so far wrong, ya know—I got more'n a thousand head a Angoras yet—some a His shepherds have to work a deal harder on Sunday than any other. Takes more persuadin' ever year to get these young rascals out come Sunday mornin'."

"You're looking fine, Mrs. Arney. You been well?" Jolly asked and immediately felt ridiculous.

"A-man. Anybody kin see I'm still as fat and healthy as I ever been, and I intend to remain this a-way, the Lord willin' in His mercy." Her great arms akimbo, she partially turned to scrutinize the crowd. "That's what I'm a-doin' here, tonight. Somebody gotta keep a eye on these here youngsters and send 'em home or they ain't never goin' to make it ta Sunday School in the morning."

"I guess it is sort of late—for these little kids," Jolly offered.

"I say a-man to that, son. It's pert' neally eleven

o'clock in the night. Well, I reckon I oughta see if I cain't drop a few hints about the time a night. It's a mercy anybody makes it ta Sunday School any more. However, as you remember from your lessons, Jolly Osment, the Lord worketh in mysterious ways." She lifted a hand in salute and moved away laboriously, her laugh rollicking above the din, leaving Jolly to ponder the applicability of her final remark.

Jolly subconsciously heard the music reach a tonic chord and stop, raggedly. A long, shrill cry broke from somewhere among the heated pack, rose to an insane pitch, suspended and then was cut short with a sharp upward yelp. The cry was repeated once or twice from diverse sides of the room. The cowboy's yell, it was used equally to drive cattle, to replace the city wolf-whistle, or as an inexplicable and carefree expression of whiskeyed joy.

While the band recessed, most of the elderly couples and little children crowded about the refreshment counter. Jolly walked away toward the doors where the stags and young couples moved out into the cooler night air, dispersed along the porch and stairs, and out among the parked cars where their presence was signaled by red dots of fire from cigarettes.

"Well, horse-patookus. Where ya been?" Luke and Babe strolled up hot and disheveled from dancing. "Where's Di?"

"Oh, she's in the can, I think."

"Who's that she was with?" asked Babe.

"Where?"

"On the dance floor."

Jolly affected a grin. "Oh, he's an old friend of mine. Bill Kemp." He laughed shortly. "I let him dance with her for a minute."

Babe winked at Luke. "If you call that *danc*ing, what they were doing." She squeezed Luke's hand, and his arm went about her waist.

"Well, old buddy, we're going to the car for a little something." Luke slapped Jolly on the shoulder. "Beer, that is," he grinned.

"OK. See you." Jolly watched them move through the knot of people on the steps. They walked arm in arm down a path between the cars, then cut to the side, toward the limousine, and out of sight. Jolly wondered fleetingly how Luke always managed so well with the girls. There was something about him that attracted and held them, but no one could have said what it was.

When the red dots of light began to arch briefly in the parking lot, and the dancers began to drift, rested and cooled, back into the hall, Jolly moved in with them.

"You got a stamp?"

"Oh, yeh. Here." He showed his hand with the purple clover.

He stood against the wall a little way from the doors and watched the dancers bunch and spread, their feet nervous on the floor. Old Cab Coon stumped by unsteadily, on his way to the band stand. As he approached, his colorless eyes, the skin pulled down in wet folds beneath them, passed over Jolly. "You bin a-goin' to church, son?" he cracked.

Jolly straightened from the wall in surprise. "Oh, yes, sir. Yes, sir. You?"

"You do the church-goin', son, and I'll do the whiskey-drinkin'." The old man wheezed past without changing his gait, intent on reaching the band stand where his wife glowered, awaiting his return.

"Well, I'll be damned," Jolly laughed. "The old goat remembered me!" Pleased, he followed the old man's progress until he stood erect on the band stand and raised his indomitable fiddle—not to his chin, but about midway on his chest. Mrs. Decker lifted her long black skirts and stepped onto the platform. With her handkerchief she dusted the piano stool, gave it a shake and sat on it, prepared to play her three-chord repertoire (in any key, in any octave) for another hour until the next intermission.

Mrs. Coon grasped the microphone, a superfluity, and announced: "Form up, folks. We're a-gonna do 'Pop Goes the Weasel' for the kiddies 'fore they gotta go home."

The young children scrambled wildly about the dance hall capturing and bartering partners until all were at least partially content with their mates. The adults moved with affected casualness among the children.

To Jolly the scene had not changed, really, in eight years. He rolled the back of his head against the polished boards of the wall. He saw the anticipation of one small boy who, wide-eyed, awaited the start of the music, oblivious of the denim-frocked girl whose hand he held from the greatest possible distance...

All around the mulberry bush
The 'possum chased the weasel

and who chewed her lip in concentration in order to better execute her skips and bobs. Mulberry bush: mulberry tree, it should be, down near the swamp, halfway to the McGowan's chicken ranch. Purple rain from shook limbs. Purple hands in galvanized buckets. Purple toes until September. Purple steaming from slatted crusts before the lamps were lighted.

Pop! goes the weasel

A funny song—funny to the West. It had traveled in consort with "Turkey in the Straw" from somewhere among distant mountains and found a compatible transplant here in the valley named from death. Funny. There had never been a 'possum nor a weasel in Skull Valley so far as anyone knew.

The tow-headed boy stamped by, breathlessly intent lest he miss the signal to pop through the opening again. His alien oxfords, dust-covered and not a little scuffed about the toes, lifted unnaturally high at each step.

"What in hell they doin' now?" asked Luke suddenly at Jolly's side, his arm monopolizing Babe's shoulders.

"It's just a play-party dance," Jolly answered and continued to roll the back of his head against the wall, gently.

"God. That'd kill me, sure," said Babe.

"You seen Di?" Luke asked.

"Nope." He faced Luke briefly as his head rolled

that way. "And wipe that goddam lipstick off your face."

"Jolly?"

"Yeh, Luke."

"You ready to cut out?"

Jolly watched the little girl in the denim frock skip by pinkly. "No matter to me. You?" He continued to roll his head over the crack between two boards.

"Well, you coming?" Luke was anxious.

"In a minute. I'll be there in a minute."

Luke and Babe disappeared through the door. Jolly let himself drift with the raucous music as it beat through the heat and whirring color of the room.

When the dance ended Jolly pushed from the wall with his shoulders. As he was about to leave, past the woman with the clover stamp, Di's voice spoke from behind him. "Jolly?"

Bill Kemp stood to one side and a little behind her. "Jolly?" Her bare shoulders and chest were damp and reflected the yellow light and changed it to glimpses of green and red. Her breath was short, perhaps from dancing.

"You ready to leave?" Jolly asked, reaching for her arm. Bill Kemp touched her other arm at the elbow, and she moved back a step.

"I'm going home with him," she said. She brushed a damp strand of hair back on her temple. "I'm sorry, Jolly—"

"But, Di. Look, we—" Jolly watched Bill Kemp's arm contract, drawing Di closer to him without moving himself forward at all. The thumb of his other hand was hooked into the front pocket of his Levis, the fingers splayed down in a token gesture of concealment.

"No," she said. "You don't know, Jolly. You just don't." For the first time, Di Carson looked cowed. She ducked her eyes and turned her face half toward Bill Kemp. As he pushed her past, he eyed Jolly from beneath his low-creased hat and winked. Jolly watched them cross the porch and go down the steps among the rows of parked cars and muddy pickup trucks.

"Bitch!" Jolly said, and the woman with the clover stamp looked up, startled. She said nothing, but she watched the boy who was vaguely familiar as he hung against a porch post a moment and then strode off into the dark.

He opened the door of the limousine and slid into the driver's seat.

"You ever find Di?" Babe asked from the back seat.

"Yeh, I found her." Jolly backed the car through a narrow space in the lot.

"Well?"

The lights picked out the gate, and he pointed the car that way.

"You just gonna *leave* without her?"

"She'll get home."

"God, she'd better," said Babe. "I'm stayin' at her house tonight. Her folks is outa town."

"If you're locked out, baby, I'll find you a bed," said Luke.

"Hm?" was the last sound Babe made for a while.

Jolly headed the car down the dirt road toward the opposite end of the valley from which they had entered.

He drove slowly for nearly a mile, not seeing the dollhouse yellow and red Santa Fe depot as he passed nor hearing the two great engines letting off excess steam from beneath their black bellies as they took water in turn from the crazy funnel that swung out on its elbow over the tracks, fifty feet from the road. He turned into a long lane darkened by interlocking cottonwood limbs. At the end of the lane he stopped the car, left the engine running, and got out to open a wood and barbed wire gate that creaked back against the fence and opened the way down the embankment to the creek bed. Jolly studied the crossing and the road reaching up the opposite bank as best he could in the beam from the car's lights. Satisfied, he walked back to the car and drove cautiously across the sand until almost to the farther bank where he stepped hard on the accelerator and bit his underlip until the heavy city car heaved up and over, its underside scraping the top edge of the bank.

"Jesus Christ," said Luke and fell silent once more.

Jolly parked the car a little distance from the creek bank, under the protective limbs of a cluster of oaks. "I'm going for a walk," he said and slammed the door shut before hearing an answer, if there was one.

He followed the two dirt tracks of the road, anticipating each turn or shallow ravine before coming upon it. The late-setting light picked out the fence line as it appeared from time to time parallel with the road. He passed by three moonstruck cows standing silent and curious among the oaks. Jolly chuckled. "You stupid cows," he said. "And I used to run like hell from your grandmothers." He chucked a stone at them and laughed aloud as they snorted and whirled, crashing into the brush, their tails high in the pale light.

At the spot in the road where it entered a tunnel of wild and ancient grape vines, Jolly paused. He peered into the blackness through which not one spark of light shone. He stepped off the road and took the short cut across an open pasture, knowing he would meet the road on the other side where it curved out of the tunnel near the elderberry bushes. Even Jamie would never pass through the grapevine tunnel at night—not to watch Jesus walk the water on the other side.

Huge against the sky he saw the circle of cottonwoods that had once formed the outer boundary of his world when he was allowed to wander alone. The trees had been planted in a circle, perhaps seventy-five feet across, as green fence posts for a corral long before Jolly's father and mother rolled into Skull Valley on the Santa Fe day coach, he restless to explore new lands, she tremorous as Tennessee moved farther and farther away. The posts had grown into trees, fed by the underground springs that flowed into the swamp, slowly wrapping their bark over the barbed wire stapled to their trunks like patient snakes gorging themselves in new spring.

Jolly left the path and walked into the circle of trees picking his way over the shattered brittle limbs that lay confused on the ground. As he passed each tree his hand remembered. When he came to a young tree standing three or four feet inside the circle, he stopped. "You're new," he said aloud. Then he laughed as if someone might have been near to hear him talking to a tree. He placed one foot on either side of the tree and ran his hands up and down over the bark. It was smoother than the older cottonwoods, but its white skin had already begun to develop the bumps and crevices common to its type. Jolly pressed his face against the cool bark, and his arms encircled the young trunk. "Goddamit," he said. His face began to throb from holding it too tightly to the bark. Beyond the circle of trees he saw the pools of water in the swamp reflect the darkling moon. As he watched, the pools began to whirl in colors. Slowly, then more frantically, the kaleidoscopic colors mixed in time to the heat of Jolly's pulse against the tree. He closed his eyes and let the pools whirl in and out among his desires. His hands moved restlessly and without reason over the white bark. Tightly, rhythmically, to the beat of the pulse in his temples he pressed all of his body against the tree.

He lay against the damp young body of the cottonwood a long time while his breath became regular again, and the pools of color settled back in the swamp. He felt his face with his fingers and could trace on his skin the marks the bark had left. He pushed back from the tree and carefully lifted and bent one leg after the other and felt gingerly the sore, raw places on the inside of his thighs.

He walked stiffly to one of the pools and squatted beside it on a wobbly hillock of grass that stood round, stump-like from the water. A person could travel a whole morning, maybe a whole day, through the swamp under the willows by stepping or jumping from one hillock to another.

The water was not cool on his face until after the breeze caught it.

Back on the road, beyond the cottonwoods and the swamp, as he approached the top of the last small hill Jolly watched the single track at his feet. When he felt he had reached the summit, a deep breath shuddered upward over his body.

He lifted his eyes toward the house and saw—nothing. Nothing but the heavenly tree forlornly genuflecting in the night air as it had done for twenty years. Where the house should have stood, its tin roof reflecting silver, Jolly could make out only a dark rectangle deep in the shagged carpet of weeds.

He scowled and shifted his direction toward where the barn should have been. Another dark rectangle; flat, dead. The water tower, too, and the windmill; they did not stand against the skyline as they should. The three peach trees—where were they? The pear tree from which he had flown and broken an arm—where was it?

Jolly sat on a granite boulder beside the road and with his chin on his hands surveyed the private ruin below him. It was not hard to re-silver the windmill so that it sparkled as it whirled water from low in the ground, or more likely, mud and bits of rotted gopher fur, because for the three hot summer months you had to haul drinking water in bellied iron barrels from some neighbor's well if you could find a truck to borrow, and you carried pails of green water from the swamp, trip after trip, for Mama to heat on the cook stove for clothes washing and Saturday baths until the late summer gully-washers foamed into the valley from the mountains, inundating everything as they came, nearly always spreading out flat clear up to the foundation of the house and leaving a dead mule or a white-faced cow to be dragged away from the sloping pasture before the house.

It was easy to re-pink the fruit trees in April in hopes the blooms would not be bitten by late frost (except those twigs that stood in blue vases on the library table). If the blossoms survived the frost, the young fruit had only to survive a water-lean summer—and wash water was some help—and the cardinals and mockingbirds and the black and yellow finches and the buckshot from Jamie's 20-gauge, and then they'd be ripe for picking. Nell Ann grumbled, but she preferred peeling any number of peaches to the risk of being blown to kingdom come by Mama's formidable pressure cooker from whence emerged enough jars of preserved fruit to last the winter, provided the winter was short-lived.

It was not too hard to rebuild the barn. The single-gabled roof rose high overhead above the empty stalls on one side and above the molded hay piles and boxes of extra Mason jars and the worn tack on the other. It was in this barn that Jamie and Jolly killed Brown Bossy through the kindness of all the barley and mash she could eat, although she lived enough hours to give birth to Beauty, a spindly-legged calf who occupied a place of esteem about the barn for the months it took to wean her of the baby bottle. Directly above the spot where Bossy gave up the ghost ran a high beam the length of the barn on which you could see gray mice scurrying most any hour of the day, and if the season were right and you pestered them with clods of dry manure, they would drop the half-eaten bloody bodies of their pink babies down on your head as if to say, "Here, take them, you want them so bad, but leave us be."

It would be harder to replant the yellow rose hedge that grew up one side of the path from the heavenly tree nearly to the front porch steps, although the nasturtium bed along the porch would riot again easily enough. It always had.

To rebuild the house itself would be next to impossible, because it would require the repossession from wherever they had been carted of each weathered plank, each rusted nail, every worn floorboard, every tin roof-patch (added at the rate of about four a year to discourage the flow of rain water inside the house). Once the materials were reassembled, the reconstruction of the house would be easier, because Jolly and Jamie and Nell Ann could tell you where every board went, how high every ceiling should be, how far it was from the back bedroom to the isinglass-eyed wood heater in the front room where pajamas were exchanged, reluctantly, for long woolen underwear every winter morning. Once the house was finished, anybody could throw the wire fence around it. Get someone to help hoist the water tank back on its timbers and realign the chicken pen—strongly this time so the coyotes will have to *work* to get in—and you'll be practically finished.

But where would you get a father? You can't play house without a mother *and* a father, even if he did only show up now and then. And what about Jamie? Nell Ann would come back and bring her own two children, but Jamie never would or if he did come back he'd never stay.

Jolly stood from the boulder, and his eyes swept over the land. He kicked a rock with his shoe and watched it tumble haltingly down the slope, sparking against other rocks, spurting tiny dust storms at each bounce until it rolled a few feet out onto the flat ground and stopped. He turned back the way he had come.

The heavenly tree bobbed in the night air as it had for twenty years.

As Jolly approached the limousine squatting like some carnivorous beast under the oak trees, Luke stepped from the car and walked to meet him at the road.

"Hi, Luke. How's the ball game? As if I couldn't see that grin even in the dark."

"Touchdown," Luke burbled. "Jesus God, Joll." His breathing was shallow and quick. The words came out on top of his breaths.

"That good, Luke?"

"You got a cigarette?"

Jolly extended the pack. "Piling sin upon sin, my brother. God, you're shaking like a leaf." Jolly held

Luke's wrist to steady the match so he could light his own cigarette. "Well? You going to tell me the details or aren't you?"

"Yeh, Joll, I will. Only there's a problem." Luke laughed nervously.

"What's the matter with you?"

"Goddamit Jolly, I *told* you we oughta bought some rubbers." Luke bit the word fiercely with his teeth.

Jolly smiled. "Don't tell me. I thought the old Santa Fe always pulled out on time."

"So did I. But it didn't this trip." Luke puffed morosely on his cigarette. It had gone out, and he flung it angrily into the dirt at his feet. "God*dam*it, Jolly, I gotta *do* something!"

"Well, what do you expect *me* to do? At least you got something for your troubles, which is a whole hell of a lot more than I did."

"You're the one made the grades in biology. What're you supposed to do in a case like this?"

Jolly snorted. "All we learned about having babies in that class was how the sperm wiggles along until it meets an egg in the uterus or somewhere, and how baby cats look inside their mother three weeks after the tom's been by."

"You're a buddy."

"Doesn't she have one of those contraptions with the hot water bottle and the tube?"

"A douche bag? No. I asked her about that. She says only married women use them."

"In that case, I'll give her one for a wedding present —about next month," Jolly laughed.

"All right, smart-ass. She's pretty worried, too. She don't know what to do, either."

"With her experience, looks like she'd *furn*ish rubbers, for chrissake. I suppose she told you she was a *vir*gin or something."

"Come on, Joll, knock it off. I'd help you think of something if you were in this boat." Luke held Jolly by both arms and gave a shake as if better to transmit his urgency. Suddenly he stopped, his hands gripping Jolly's upper arms. His eyes grew wide and he grinned, his face level with Jolly's.

"Embalming fluid!" he exclaimed.

"What? Are you some kind of a nut?"

"That's it! Embalming fluid! That'll kill anything," Luke cried happily.

"Including Babe Wooten?" Jolly asked.

"No, it won't hurt her none. I don't think it will, anyhow." A small frown passed over his brow.

"What's she gonna do, drink it?"

"No, moron. We'll hook her up to the embalming machine and give her the red tube in the you-know-where!"

"Oh, Jesus, Luke. You sure that'll work?"

"Well, we gotta try something, haven't we? Come on. Let's roll." Luke executed a sprightly kick in the weeds. "Squirrel!"

"Ouch! Wait a minute, Luke. You going to put her up on the table in the preparation room? I don't think she'll like that much. Besides, you know, she might have company."

"I'll work on that problem on the way home. You drive."

"What am I, a goddam chauffeur? See you don't work on another baby, dad."

At two-thirty in the morning the black Chrysler edged to the curb in front of Di Carson's house. The three, Jolly, Luke, and Babe Wooten, each noticed the battered pick-up truck standing in the driveway, but no one spoke of it. No lights shone from anywhere in the house, not from either story. If there was any life in the house (and likely there was) its porticoed face gave no hint of it.

As so often before, Jolly—sprawled sleepily over most of the back seat—watched Luke say goodnight to a girl at her front porch, although this night they were not really visible because the moon had dipped far in the west. The goodnight was a brief one, doubtless because even a prolonged kiss would be anticlimactic at that point in a night of bliss, alarm, or disappointment, depending on whose point of view you saw it through.

The brisk pace Luke had set for himself in the night had slackened considerably by the time he returned to his father's car, which itself had encompassed this night a new experience far removed from its usual role of carrying bereaved families to and from the cemetery.

"Tired, my prodigal son?"

"Jeez." Luke slumped into the driver's seat. "Jeez," he repeated to himself.

"You ought to have worked up a sizable appetite by

now. I'll buy," said Jolly, his long legs crossed at the ankles over one of the folding seats.

Luke started the car tiredly and swung it around in the street, headed for Freddy's.

"I can't figure why she got so damned modest at the last minute." Jolly felt the hysterical giggle rising from his stomach. "I'd've given my left gonad to watch Young Doctor Meaders in operation tonight."

"No, you wouldn't've," said Luke, quietly.

"Maybe you could go into business, Luke." It was coming now. There wasn't any stopping it. "You could buy your own little all-purpose embalming and automatic douche machine." The words were hard put to get around the giggles.

"All right, wise guy. All right."

"Maybe you could get a portable one. Do they make portable ones? You could plug it into the cigarette lighter or somewhere—"

"Knock it off, Joll." Luke's tired voice had an edge around it.

"—and that would save flopping their butts on that cold table. You could make a hell of a lotta money. You really could." Jolly stopped to laugh. "I'll be your manager. Can I be your manager, Luke?"

"Jolly, goddamit, shut up!"

"We could have little cards printed up. Business cards. What'll we say on 'em, Luke? 'Bring your troubles to us: Dead or alive we fix them up.' How's that? Or how about, 'Expert Semen Sweeping: After Hours Service, No Extra Charge for Home Calls,' or—"

"Jolly. I'm warning you." Luke slowed the car.

"—'Tubes Cleaned While You Wait.' At five bucks a throw, plus transportation costs, of course, we could really clean up in this friggin' town. We could give out the cards at school—sort of like another library card—and maybe we could sneak into Doogle's and poke holes in all the prophylactics and then leave one of the little cards in the package." His words rose in spasms of sound.

Luke drove the car in Freddy's parking lot and swung it to the far side, away from the lights. He pulled the hand brake deliberately and turned off the key. For a moment he rested his forehead on his hands that gripped the wheel, shutting out the sounds of Jolly's hysteria. Then he walked into the restaurant. "Two hamburgers and two coffees. To go," he told the waitress.

EIGHT

THE car had been parked across the street and a little down from the house more than an hour ago, in a place past the light where the mulberry branches arched over the sidewalk and farther, ten feet over the street. The car was some dark color, black or maybe maroon, but it would have been impossible to say which, parked that way in the black shade of the leaves.

Jamie left the car almost as soon as it slipped into the shade. He stood beside it a time while nothing showed but the repeated sudden bright-orange pin of light that glowed, then arched down and dimmed. Finally, the pin of light skittered five or six feet over the pavement, shooting tiny, frustrated fractures of orange that died instantly. He crossed the street diagonally into the lamplight and then into the dark again as he turned up the overgrown path between the two pines. He stood there with his hands jammed into the front pockets of his tight, black pants and faced the house in the way a man watches something because it's there—to hold his eyes—while his mind is somewhere else. He did not move for a long time except to cup the light of a match to his face twice or three times, and to shift his weight from one foot to the other as quietly as a hunter standing in oak cover waiting at dawn for a deer to cross. When the beams from the approaching car first caught the lilac bushes, Jamie turned his head toward them and watched the car come fast up the street, its lights flicking quick dapples over his pale face.

Jolly stood for a moment to watch Luke squeal the big car out into the street before he turned up the path. He saw the figure beside the pine an instant before it spoke.

"Jolly," the voice said, almost too quietly to hear.

Jolly recognized that voice and knew he recognized it before he jumped, but he could not stop his heart from thumping once, any more than he could stop the small yelp.

"Jamie!"

Jamie laughed, low and throaty. "Hi, Jolly." He stayed where he was, there in the shadow of the pine and lilac.

"Jeez, Jamie. What're you doing here? Jeez." Jolly stepped across the path near the tree. "It's about time. Where the hell have you been all this time? Jamie, why—"

Jamie laughed, and his hand entered the dim light to touch Jolly's shoulder and then the back of his neck. "You still ask questions. I could ask you what the hell you're doing coming home now, at this time of night."

"It's not so late," Jolly grinned. His hands went first to his front pockets, then settled in the back ones. "You used to be as late. Or maybe not come in—"

"OK," Jamie said. "OK. Here, sit down." He squatted on his heels. Jolly sat beside him, on a rock.

He heard Jamie rustling a cigarette package. "You smoke?"

"Some. Yeh, I smoke some. Not too much, but Mom—"

"Look, I don't care. You got any? I'm out."

Jolly felt in his own shirt pocket. "Yeh, sure, Jamie. I have some." The pack was jammed in his pocket. He yanked at it. "Just a minute," he said. "I've got some right here." His fingers plucked at the pocket. "Goddam things are stuck."

"Take it easy," Jamie said. "Here." He reached his hand into Jolly's pocket where all the confusion was just as surely as if he could see in the dark and took out the pack. "You want one?"

He had thought he was going to say yes. "No," he said.

"Here."

"No. You keep them."

"I got more in the car." Jamie touched Jolly's arm with the cigarette package.

"You keep them, Jamie," he said. And then he laughed, "I'll just have to hide them when I get in." He stopped talking when he felt Jamie's hand replace the pack in his shirt pocket.

When the brief, cupped light flared, Jolly watched it outline the front part of his brother's face in profile. With his cheeks sucked in to draw the smoke and his eyes squinted with the black, heavy eyebrows pulled deep, he could have been a stranger, except for something there in his face that was familiar, but that seemed to belong to someone else.

They sat that way together a long time, neither speaking, while Jamie automatically smoked the cigarette and Jolly concentrated on keeping his hands and feet still by folding his arms and leaning them forward on his knees. Somewhere behind them in the dry leaves a cricket took up his squalid chanting again and was answered by a dimmer voice up the path nearer the house. It was funny how people you knew well smelled the same, even after two years and after things change so much. Jamie smelled as he had forever. A little damp and leatherish, only now the leather smell would be from automobile upholstery. And the same hair oil that was some too sweet and was supposed to keep Jamie's black curls from falling out but didn't. The tobacco smell was right, too, only milder, as old as the leather. Jolly thought of the times, back in the country, when he carefully filched their father's cigarettes or gathered butts from along the roadside to save for Jamie who would smoke anything, including grapevine and Bull Durham.

"You going in to see Mom? She'll be awake."

"No. Not tonight." Jamie ground the cigarette out in the dirt beside his boot.

"Where've you been, Jamie. What've you been doing since last time?"

Jamie laughed. He did not say anything, not for a while, but the short, brittle sound stilled Jolly's question. "Oh, I've been here and there, Joll. Mostly in hell," he added.

"What?"

"Skip it."

"Jamie, tell me about—well, you know. You must've gotten a lot of girls and all." He laughed. "With that pecker you've got, you—"

"Don't talk like that. What do you think you are? And you're not my goddam confessor. So shut up." He reached out his hand to Jolly's shoulder. "Aw, sit down and wait a minute."

Yes, he guessed he could tell the kid a couple of tales. He could tell him one tale, all right. One that would make him curl up his hind-end and run. The one that made him sick to his stomach still to think about. And Mandy. The kid had probably eyed that himself. He'd seen the high-school boys twitch and go blind-eyed dumb when she took their orders at Freddy's. Well, that wasn't worked out, either. But he had had to admit, the kid—the baby—was funnier than hell. And she was all right, too. After that first night he had been able to stay, and with the lights off he had been able to forget about the little boy. She really was all right. At least she didn't bitch about anything, and she sure didn't have it so good. If anybody could appreciate that fact, he was the one. A big pecker, yeah. And the big peckers shall inherit the earth and fill it with fools and nightmares.

"You want to talk, Jolly, go on. I don't have anything to say. You never did tell me where you've been so late."

Jolly told him. He told him more than he meant to, about Di Carson and the dance and about Bill Kemp. He didn't say anything about what Luke and Babe Wooten had done. He felt Jamie's eyes on him, although he couldn't see him. He talked a long time until he had said it all, nearly. When his voice ran down to nothing, Jamie reached over to his pocket and fished out another cigarette and lit it before he said anything.

"You swear a lot," Jamie said. The orange light showed for a moment his fingers and the lower part of his face. "Why'd you take that kind of girl?"

Jolly scraped a place in the dirt and needles with his heel. "I thought you'd get the idea," he said.

"I did," Jamie said. "You sixteen now, Joll?"

"Yeh," Jolly answered morosely, as if sixteen were the year of the plague. "How old were you, Jamie?"

"When?"

"You know when, goddamit, Jamie."

Jamie laughed, louder than before, but still too quietly to be heard far. Then he was silent again. "I don't know. Younger than you, I guess. But what difference does it make."

"What difference? It makes a whole hell of a lot of difference. To me."

"That's the point," Jamie said.

"What?"

"The difference." Jamie's hand lay on Jolly's knee, there in the dark by the pine. "You're not me, Jolly."

"I know that."

"No, you don't. You don't know that at all. You think just because— Well, forget it. I can't help you any more than I can help me. That's all."

"Don't go, Jamie."

"I got to."

Jolly stood. "No, you don't, Jamie. Can't we talk some more? I want—"

"I'll be around. Not any more, now." Jamie moved in the shadow, but silently. "And, Jolly?"

"Yeh? Hey!"

"Hold still. Listen. You don't know—you're better. You're better."

A moving branch tipped the pale light over Jolly's face for an instant, but he could still not see the other face. He only felt the strong arms on his own. "What do you mean? I guess I don't know what anybody means."

"Just shut up and listen. You know it killed our old man, don't you?" Jamie watched as the light tipped again. "No."

"What, Jamie?"

Jamie laughed, low, mirthlessly. "No, you wouldn't know. Forget that, Jolly. And forget what you're trying to do. Just let it go."

"Wait. Wait a minute, Jamie. Tell me, Jamie. Tell me what—"

"Hush," he whispered. Jolly felt his fingers, light yet strong and thin, cover his mouth. "Hush. I'm going to tell you sometime, Jolly, some things I haven't even said to myself. Wait. Not now. Not now. You listening?"

Jolly nodded, but he couldn't have said anything if he had wanted to, with those fingers growing tighter against his mouth. He could feel Jamie close to him, so close he could hear him breathe. So close that even in the shadow of the pine and lilac he could see Jamie's face dimly emerge, and he wondered at its whiteness.

"You were right to let that one go. Even if you could have stopped her, you were right to let that one go. That's no good. Sure, I know it's great to think about it, and it's great to do it. But it's no good this way. You've got a hard on every night when you go to bed and every morning when you wake up and half a dozen times in between. And I know, it won't wear out. Dammit, Jolly, you're only a kid!" Jamie's voice was close and fierce. "You're only a kid," he said. "And that's not what matters at all. What's on your mind—that's not what matters." He felt Jolly's body flinch. He relaxed his hold and stepped back in the deeper shadow by the tree. "Sorry," he said and was quiet.

Again he began. "You don't know what I'm talking about, do you."

"No, I don't," Jolly said. "What do you expect me to do? Tie a red ribbon around it and save it for my old age?"

"Don't be a smart-ass all your life."

"You sound like you're talking about love, for chrissake. I'm not talking about that. I don't even believe in it, anyway."

"Well, you got a lot to learn. More than I figured. And I guess I'm not the one to teach it to you. I'm going now," he said.

Jolly watched him pass through the light from the street lamp and into the dark again beneath the overhanging mulberry branches.

NINE

LATER the same morning, despite the fact that sleep had not come to him until after the pine outside his bedroom had greened in the dawn, Jolly walked to church with his mother. He did it more to dissuade her temper than for any latent religious consciousness. And she had enjoyed very little more sleep than he, lying awake until his footsteps sounded on the path, until she had heard the caution of the back door, and felt, rather than saw, the bare light spring against the stove and the table and the ancient green washer. She heard her younger boy undress clumsily in the dark living room and listened to the long-familiar snap of the board between the kitchen and the bathroom. She heard the toilet flush, water running in the sink, the snap of the board again.

"Lord have mercy," she prayed, and then she slept the three hours until it would be time to be up stirring around.

She had not spoken more than was necessary to disunite Jolly from his bed and inform him his breakfast was ready. Mattawilde Osment had never been one to have it out with her children, or anybody else, except perhaps the greengrocer when he tried to foist inferior tomatoes or mustard greens on her. Her tight-lipped anger was doubtless inbred as part of the formula for rearing proper Southern girls in a family abundant in everything—including correct ante-bellum genealogy—except money.

Or it may have developed from twenty-five years of following in her husband's tracks over most of the United States and a good portion of Canada, seeing him mostly on station platforms, until he settled for the last time in Skull Valley. Their years together in the Southwest were peaceful ones; so much so in fact, that Mattawilde gave birth to her third child at the age of forty-eight and was pretty put out about it—not that she didn't want the child, but because both she and the doctor in Cortez thought it was a tumor for the first five months, which put her rather far behind with her layette.

She had been the only one of her family to travel farther than Knoxville, with the exception of the youngest boy, Robert, who turned renegade and went up North to preach for the Methodists.

She limped from the refrigerator to the stove, giving the brunt of her anger to a black iron skillet she had had longer than she had Jolly. The limp was forty-six years old. She acquired it at the age of seventeen when in a black-eyed fury she had pitted her matched mules against the team of a particularly contemptible young man from Nashville with whom she was seasonally in love. Her buggy, although not far in the rear at the time, overturned, and the off-mule kicked the bone in her leg to smithereens. The city fellow kept going.

Beside his plate Jolly found two items that belied

his mother's anger, if nothing else did. A tall glass of tomato juice. That would be because she believed two beers made you drunk, and she had read somewhere that tomato juice was the only antidote. A nearly empty pack of Lucky Strikes. That was to show Jolly he had forgotten to hide them early this morning, and that she was on to his tricks. Jolly stuffed the package into his bathrobe pocket and picked up the glass of juice.

"Here's your eggs." She slid three fried eggs onto his plate and a half-dozen slices of bacon. "Hustle up. They's hot cakes in a minute."

"Aw, Mom. You know I hate big breakfasts." Jolly poked the center of an egg and watched the yolk spread under the bacon.

"Hum." That was her method of punishment—big breakfasts. It would serve him right, staying out all the live-long night, galavanting heaven knows where. "Serves you right," she said, pouring batter into the skillet.

Nothing more was said by either over breakfast. Later they emerged dressed for church, she from the bedroom, he from the bathroom, and met in the living room. He scowled at the morning comics and she at the clock until it read twenty of eleven, precisely. She stood from her rocker, ran a pin through her hat at a jaunty angle, picked up her Bible and purse and said, "It is time."

The walk to the Morningside Baptist Church helped alleviate her feelings, as Jolly was sure it would. She was secretly proud to show her tall son to the Sunday morning world, and besides, the walk gave her a chance to inspect the progress of everybody's iris and lilac. She had theorized for years, when neighbors stopped to comment on her own flowers, that "A body couldn't grow a hill a beans in this dirt. All's I do is just scratch around, just scratch around," although when her brothers and sisters urged her return to Tennessee she reckoned she had too much dust and cactus in her hide to ever appreciate jasmine or magnolias again.

At the doors of the church the ladies gathered to one side, ostensibly to get a better view of, and greet, any newcomers. The men gathered dourly a little distance away, talking about whatever noncontroversial topics there are left to discuss within the shadow of a Baptist Church. The young people, those who couldn't escape being neither fish nor fowl, entered the church so that they could get the choice seats as far back as possible under the balcony where it was unlikely anyone had ever heard a word spoken in a normal voice from the pulpit.

"Mother, let's go on in," said Jolly, offering her his arm.

"Just a minute, Jolly-Bo. I want to speak to Miz Edhols." She drew Jolly with her.

"Hello, Mattawilde. Jolly. My, he's still growin' like a weed." Jolly winced. "I was sayin' to my Billy this mornin'—you know my Billy just ad*mires* Jolly. Thinks the world an' all of him. He truly does."

Mama eyed Jolly significantly for a second.

"Wants to sing like him, and everything. Course, my Billy's goin' in the ministry. He's already made up his mind and seems there ain't nothin' me nor Homer can do about it—not that we'd be wantin' to, you understand. He does have a fine voice, don't he?"

"Who?" asked Mama, her lips thin.

"Why, Billy! A course he's not as old as your Jolly, but when he *is*—" She winked at Jolly, and he fluttered the makings of a smile, hoping she hadn't expected him to wink back. "—he'll be somethin' to behold. Well, you gotta fine Christian boy, too, Mattawilde. Lord bless us."

You old bat, thought Jolly. You and your snot-nosed Billy. I wish he could have been along last night. He might have learned something—enough to curl *your* ears.

"Thank you, Mrs. Edhols. You coming, Mother?"

"You run along. I'll be there directly," she said, turning to greet skinny Mrs. Fries.

Jolly had to shake no less than fourteen hands on his way up the stairs to the inside doors. These were the elected Greeters and Ushers, both active and emeritus, the former group ladies, the latter, men. At the very top of the stairs he extracted his hand from a lady's cotton grip and grasped a man's.

"Good morning, Jolly."

Jolly looked in the intense eyes of the preacher, a dark young man of less than thirty who had been in his present church only a year. "Just like a grand reception line, isn't it," he smiled.

"Yeh," Jolly laughed. "I feel like Queen Elizabeth, or something. Ah— how are you, Mr. Cramer?"

"I'm fine, thanks. You? We haven't seen you here

lately, have we? You haven't forgotten us, I hope?" He still held Jolly's hand in his own white one, smiling. He was an acutely handsome man, Jolly thought, startled at the revelation, except he was too short. Jolly felt nervous looking down at adults, which kept him nervous a good deal of the time.

"No, sir. I'm fine. Well—" he looked toward the people gathering after him on the stairs and attempted to disengage his hand without yanking.

"We haven't heard you practicing the piano lately." The minister's dark eyes smiled directly into, albeit slightly up into, Jolly's.

Jolly blushed. "How did you know about that? I didn't think anyone knew I came in here to practice."

"I've been here—back in my office—when you came in. I used to enjoy hearing you play. But you haven't been here in a long time." The man lifted his brows, awaiting an answer.

"No. No, sir, I haven't," Jolly said. "Well, we're holding up the line." He pulled his hand free and ducked into the sanctuary.

The preferred seats under the balcony were all pretty well taken by fat Ron Corcoran and his followers, so Jolly sat at the outside on the last row of regular seats. You had to have a good night's sleep to keep up with Ron's illustrated hymnals and running comments on the state of affairs as they occurred in the Morningside Baptist Church on Sunday morning.

From where Jolly sat he had a reasonable view of the whole church, and he began his old game of identifying its members by the backs of their heads. The church seated exactly a hundred and forty-four people (not counting the balcony, which was never used except for the ethereal sounds the choir affected from there at Christmas pageants, and the prized seats under the balcony) as Jolly well knew from past Sundays when he had counted one row across, nine, and the rows back, eight, multiplied, seventy-two, times two, a hundred and forty-four. Identifying the regular members of the congregation wasn't difficult but it occupied a certain portion of an hour.

Near the front on the far right, so his good ear would be attuned, sat Brother Able Peckham, who seemed to have been sitting precisely there since shortly after the Crucifixion. Beside him sat his tiny speckled wife, who would be asleep as soon as the singing was through, the two cherries in her summer hat bobbing restfully as she snoozed. In her usual place, Mrs. Hacy's broad arms were flung in either direction along the back of the pew, the better to reach any member of the brood under her discipleship. She believed no child was too young to attend Sunday morning service if properly attended by resounding snaps on the head at judicious moments.

Luke passed by, down the aisle, steered by his mother, whose jaw was set peculiarly. He exchanged a brief glance with Jolly, but it was enough to say, "Don't call today. In fact, it'll likely be a year before things settle down at my house."

Jolly's own mother came into the church and got caught in the choice of sitting beside Mrs. Shiverly, whom she "loathed and despised" or beside Anita

Meaders, Luke's mother. Jolly was relieved to see her sit beside Mrs. Shiverly, because at least *they* wouldn't talk.

Breathless, the Sanic Sisters flowed into their pew after first shooshing away some strangers who hadn't any idea there were reserved seats. Once settled, the Sisters checked the hymn numbers on the board and opened their personal morocco-bound hymnals, held them forward, prepared to sing. When the Sanic Sisters were in attendance, and they hadn't missed a Sunday in anyone's memory, there wasn't any sense in the song leader or pianist trying to set a tempo, because there wasn't anyone (outside of, perhaps, Mississippi Arney of Skull Valley) who could out-sing the Sisters in volume. A new minister always tried to outwit them at first by selecting obscure hymns with which they might not be familiar, but that always turned out to be a trio—the minister himself and the Sanic Sisters—because unless it was written by Mary Baker Eddy there wasn't a hymn they hadn't pretty well set to memory.

At eleven o'clock the door on the dais (on which hung the record of Sunday School attendance and offerings) swung open and the choir filed in. They were outfitted in maroon robes with white collars. The ladies deposited their purses at their feet as they sat. "Oh, no," groaned Jolly to himself. "Old man Rainey's going to sing." Cleve Rainey graced the choir four or five times a year when he felt up to a solo, and his presence there should be publicized ahead of time, a good number of the congregation agreed, so they could stay away. Cleve was pushing sixty, and his tenor voice had given up twenty years earlier. Behind Cleve Rainey strode Mrs. Edhols' Billy, pompous as a bantam rooster, a regular member of the adult choir, a fact Mrs. Edhols was pointing out to her neighbor.

From the door at the other side of the dais (on which hung the hymn numbers and scripture reading) entered the minister, who had spirited himself around the church in order to enter there. He surveyed his audience and then sat in his plush carved chair before the camouflaged baptismal tank—the swimming pool, as it was known by the irreverent young. The congregation began to fidget and crane to eye a particular vacant seat. There wasn't any use to begin the services until Brother Ep Edward Clydefield occupied that pew. Once, a number of years ago, "Holy, Holy, Holy" was just at the amen point when Ep Edward entered, and he stood right where he was and made them do the whole thing over again from the beginning. The membership got the idea thereafter that services didn't begin—if they were to maintain any decorum at all—until Brother Ep Edward had arrived. And Brother Ep Edward was the foremost cause of the mortgage's being burned ten years ahead of schedule.

"Brother Ep Edward ain't arrived," whispered a lady beside Jolly, as if everyone didn't know.

At five minutes past eleven, the old gentleman arrived at his pew in a regular suite of ushers. He wore his white perforated summer shoes and a white Panama suit (the only one ever known in Cortez) and handed his white straw to a solicitous usher. At his appearance the pianist broke into the run-through of "Holy," and the congregation rose to its feet. To a visitor it would be hard to distinguish to whom the song was directed, God or Ep Edward.

As the service droned on, through the Morning Prayer, the Scripture Lesson, and the Weekly Announcements, Jolly felt his eyelids begin their protest. The room was hot, and the overhead fans whirled at just the right speed to mesmerize a person. Finally, the choir stood to sing the anthem, an expurgated setting of something by Handel, but the solo passage lent itself well to Cleve Rainey's singing because you couldn't tell the trills and runs from the natural wobbles in his voice.

The sermon began. Jolly settled farther into his seat, determined that by listening carefully he could stay awake for thirty-five more minutes.

"Ladies and gentlemen; brothers and sisters," Harold Cramer began in his resonant, eleven-o'clock voice, "this morning I have chosen as my text, Jeremiah, Chapter Six, Verse Fifteen." He paused as Bibles rustled, no one wishing to be the last to find the passage. ("Old Testament," murmured the lady beside Jolly.) "I read: 'Were they ashamed when they had committed abomination? nay, they were not at all ashamed, neither could they blush: therefore they shall fall among them that fall: at the time that I visit them they shall be cast down, saith the Lord.' A-men."

"That's right, Brother!" shouted Able Peckham, which may have indicated he was there when it happened.

Jolly didn't remember the verse in question, but he could tell from its tone that the congregation was in for it this morning. He shifted his gaze to the back of Luke's head. From there he looked to the young girls in the choir, whose faces served as mirrors of Luke. He discovered Netty Alan blushing pink above her choir robe. So Luke was winking at Netty today. "Blush, poor girl," thought Jolly, "but you'll never make it in the Blue Goose."

At twelve fifteen exactly, the Sanic Sisters let go their final tone, reluctantly, Harold Cramer rushed to the back of the church to begin shaking everyone's hand for the second time, and Jolly Osment fell in love.

As he turned into the aisle, there she was. It was as simple as that. There she was. There she was stepping between her father (who had concealed her before) and mother directly across the aisle. Her eyes met his squarely without hesitation, and the heat lifted from the room as clearly as if a window had opened itself to spring. She returned his smile, and still stepping between her parents, she ignored the preacher's proffered hand, and Jolly watched incredulously as her white sailor hat bobbed down the stairs.

"Excuse me," said the lady behind him.

"Oh, excuse *me,* ma'am." He rushed ahead of her.

"You will come in to play, won't you?" the preacher was asking.

"Yes. Yes, sir. I enjoyed—I liked your sermon." Jolly watched the hat bob through the front doors. He pulled on his hand.

"Thank you, Jolly," Harold Cramer said. "We'll see you?"

"Yes," he said aloud, and to himself, "Let go, let *go.*"

"And Jolly?" the preacher persisted.

"Yes, sir?"

"Their name is Van Dearen. That's D-e-a-r-e-n."

"Thank *you,* Mr. Cramer!" The hat was no longer to be seen. Jolly clattered down the stairs but checked himself prudently before rushing hell-bent into the sunlight, lest he appear anxious. The girl was just ducking into the back seat of a car. Her mother and father were already in the front. "Damn," said Jolly. What was a person to do? You can't just go rushing up to complete strangers and say "Excuse me, sir, but I want to stare at your daughter."

The sedan backed out into the street, stopped for a moment, then nosed away, around the corner, the white sailor hat nearly the last thing to go out of sight.

Jolly grouched against the hot stone church and waited for his mother. She arrived in time, with Mr. and Mrs. Favor, who had offered them a ride home in their car.

"Unless you'd rather walk, Jolly?"

"No ma'am. I'd rather ride." And that was the truth. It was too hot to walk if you didn't have to, and not only from the sun.

"All's we're having is some leftovers," Mattawilde spoke from the kitchen, later. "But I think I'll serve them in the dining room. It's cooler."

"OK with me," said Jolly.

"Well, you can't sit in the dining room in nothing but your pants. Run put a shirt on. And some *shoes.* I don't care if we are the only ones left around here. Besides, it's Sunday."

"All right, Mom. Anything you say. Mom?" Jolly called with his head in the closet, "did you see those new people at church? The man and the woman. And the girl?"

"Was she the one with the green summer straw?"

"No. It was white. One of those big, broad-brimmed ones." Jolly paused. "Oh, you mean the woman?"

"Yes. Who'd you think I meant?"

"I didn't notice what she was wearing. Their name is Van Dearen. That's D-e-a-r-e-n."

"I know," she said.

"How'd *you* know?" Jolly came into the kitchen, buttoning his shirt.

"Well, don't look at me like I haven't got good sense." She made another trip from the kitchen to the table. "I asked around." And that was more than Jolly had had the mind to do.

"I might have known. Isn't she pretty?"

"Who?"

"The girl. You know who I mean."

"Here, carry these." She moved deliberately into the dining room (which was really only the far end of the living room) with Jolly close behind. "I reckon I didn't notice."

"What do they do? Where do they live? Do you suppose they're real *strict* Baptists?"

"Wouldn't hurt you none to know some real strict

ones. And I don't know their whole life history. Set down and have your lunch."

Jolly poked among the cold chicken parts until he found a thigh. It had lain overnight at the bottom of the dish and had a thin edge of white grease on it. He began to scrape the grease away with his fork.

"How is it you never liked the drumstick? You're the only one a my children never fought for the drumstick."

"That's because I was deprived as a child," said Jolly, scrutinizing the chicken thigh.

"What do you mean deprived? Wasn't anyone in *my* house ever deprived or went hungry. Not that I ever knew of." She pulled off a small piece of meat and chewed it delicately. At sixty-four Mattawilde Osment was in fair health, but her teeth were wearing down. "Never did have a true bite," she had often said.

"Oh, Mom, I mean there's ordinarily only two drumsticks on a chicken, right?"

"Never heard different."

"You ever heard of two characters, formerly from these parts, name of Jamie and Nell Ann?"

His mother tidied her lips with a linen napkin. Her brown eyes shot past Jolly to the pictures on the buffet. "Don't be gettin' sassy, young man," she said in a voice that was clear sign she was changing the subject. "Eat some a these asparagus. They're right tender."

"Cold? Jeez, they're bad enough hot."

"You used to like them, as I recall. I don't know what gets into you sometimes. Lord knows; I don't."

"Mother, I used to like to *cut* asparagus when we

grew it. I never liked to eat it." True, fresh asparagus spears, just six or seven inches high, cut clean and nice and made you feel you *had* something. Not like picking tomatoes, or pulling radishes or turnips or anything that had to be yanked, or that came out of the dirt unwillingly.

"What you grinnin' like a chessy-cat for?"

"Nothing, Mom." Every time he saw asparagus he thought of Jamie's comment ages ago about their being phallic symbols. The comparison would have meant nothing, of course, had not Jamie continued with one of his famous explanations, which were seldom accurate but always graphic. Accurate or not, Jolly never ate asparagus with what anyone could have called relish, afterward.

"Jolly-Bo."

"Hum?" He watched her slice an asparagus spear into bite sizes.

"I been meaning to talk to you about Jamie." Her eyes, peering above her glasses, concentrated on the asparagus, which meant she was approaching a topic she would rather put off.

"What about Jamie?"

"Have you seen him and didn't tell me?"

"Yes. I saw him last night." He watched her lips begin to tighten.

"Was that you and him I heard talking out in front right before you came in? I thought so." She glanced up at him. "What did he tell you?"

"What do you mean, what did he tell me? We just

talked. About things." He lined up the chicken bones to one side of his plate.

"Now, I want to know. What things."

"Aw, Mom. Just things, that's all."

"Did he tell you anything about himself? You know, where he's been and what he's been up to?"

"No. I asked him, but he wouldn't tell me anything. Why? What's the matter?"

She reached for his plate to stack on her own. "I don't know." She tk'd her tongue and repeated, "I don't know. Something. I'm worried."

Jolly threw down his napkin. "What's there about him to worry over? He hasn't been home ten minutes his whole life, it seems to me. Not when anybody needed him or wanted him. He's been here a whole damn—a whole darn week and I get about a half hour." He scraped his chair back from the table.

"Don't get on your high horse, Jolliff. If Jamie doesn't want to talk, he's got reason. You let him alone, you hear?"

"Let him alone! Look, I don't want his whole crazy *life,* I just want— Oh, forget it. I don't want anything." He sat on the sofa to tie his shoe laces.

"Where you going?"

"Out."

"In this heat? Seems to me you'd love and appreciate a nap today, what with all the galavantin' you been doing lately. And haven't you got some last-minute school work to do?"

"I'll do it later." At the door he turned. "Mom, you don't know where he's staying, do you?"

She shook her head.

He closed the front door and jammed his hands in his pockets and faced the proposition of walking to Doogle's in the heat. He wouldn't worry about anything at all, not until he got to the drugstore and cooled off, and then he could use the telephone there if he decided to.

Cortez wasn't up to much early on a Sunday afternoon. The streets were nearly empty of traffic, except for a few cars headed out Sierra Road toward the country club and another afternoon of golf or bridge or gin and tonic. The front shades were pulled in most of the houses, and even the trees drooped and nodded as if they also would take an hour or two off from growing.

A green Ford convertible raked down the hill past Jolly, its nose dipped forward, pipes popping. "Fingers!" Guppy called, and the five or six bodies laughed by, nothing but bare skin showing above the edge of the car, on their way to the lake.

Jolly waved. "Hello, Hero." He paused to watch them out of sight. The seniors had finished their exams the week before, and Guppy was graduating at last. He could well spend the day (and the night) at the lake in celebration. He had just been awarded the healthiest scholarship of anyone in his class to play football for the university. On the strength of that and his size, and the footwork of his coaches, he would be given a diploma the following week along with the eggheads who couldn't afford a raked green convertible with twin pipes and twin spots and mirrors and green-and-white-striped leather upholstery. Just how Guppy came to afford the car wasn't certain, although a number of people had wondered, briefly. It was doubtful his ten-year-widowed mother could have bought it for him, what with only her six women tenants in the cupolaed and turreted white house that stood opposite the old grammar school. She had had the house chopped up into small apartments after her husband died, and she had tried to lighten the rooms and cheer the naturally morose exterior with white paint and pots of red geraniums. But the geraniums in the window boxes seldom lived because over there, that close to Maricopa Street and the noisy playground, it was hard to get genteel tenants who would give care to geraniums. Mostly the ones who came to live there were secretaries and beauty operators. They were all flighty-restless, apt to move closer to downtown after three or four months, so that a person couldn't depend on having any tenants at all except for the two over-thirty women who taught across the street and shared the expense of one apartment and whom she would not have had back at all this year, because they sometimes acted strangely, if she could have picked and chosen.

Guppy helped around the place, mending stairs, or mowing the lawns, or painting—the things a man would have to be hired to do next year when he left for the university. She had worried some the last couple of years about her son in the house with those flighty-restless girls, and she had tried to see that things that needed fixing in their rooms got done during the day. If there was something at night, a leaky faucet, or a stuck toilet or window, she went along, too, and chatted about the geraniums or the cost of plumbing. With the schoolteachers it was different, of course. They were finicky about things in their apartment, more so, probably, than they had a right to be, not paying any more rent than they paid, and they had the only keys to the lock that had been changed on their door (heaven alone knew what she'd do if she ever really *had* to get in there), which meant that Guppy—Benjy—would have to go up there at night if anything needed fixing, when he would sooner be with his own friends, but then, after he had unstuck their toilet, or whatever it was, they would help him with his homework, and she could go on to bed more than a little thankful that the boy wasn't out chasing around town.

When the two teachers told Mrs. Gusperson that they wanted to buy the green car for Guppy for graduation, she was bewildered and touched. It wasn't, after all, a really *new* car, they had explained. She wasn't sure it was the right thing to do, but maybe a boy who didn't have any father and who had to help around the house instead of working for money deserved a little something more than she could provide, and, well, if they really wanted to do it, she guessed they would anyway, whether she had anything to say about it or not. But she thought she'd be able to have their apartment done over with that blue paper and new curtains this summer while they were gone.

Jolly and Guppy had developed an unspoken mutual respect since Guppy had learned that Jolly lately listened when he talked (and could diagram two or three senior sentences in the hall between classes), and Jolly had learned that whatever he might not be, Guppy was constant. Guppy was proud of the green Ford and embarrassed by it at first, until he had one day tried incoherently to explain its reason for being to Jolly, who hadn't asked, and found he couldn't, but more than that he realized for the first time that even if he could speak as well as he wished he could, even if he explained the whole crazy thing, it wouldn't make sense.

Jolly cut across the plaza on the courthouse square. Several families of early tourists who didn't know of the good picnic spots were eating hot dogs and drinking pop and sleeping, their children flitting over the fresh lawns like bits of bright paper in the wind.

He stopped beside the goldfish pond, black-railed more for the safety of the fish than the children. From the fountain, green and slime-coated, the water splashed sporadically, keeping the fish in a state of constant agitation. Jolly watched for Old Whitey, a giant by goldfish standards and bleached white from age and poor sunlight, to come to the edge of the pond.

"There you are, you old scavenger," Jolly laughed. "And I haven't got anything for you." He tore a match from its packet and struck it. When it blazed he dropped it directly upon the fish, who seemed to hang suspended on an invisible wire just beneath the surface. The fish didn't flinch as the match hissed onto the water. "Can't fool you, can I," Jolly said.

He left the pond and stopped to gaze at the bronze statue of Teddy Roosevelt presumably charging San

Juan Hill, sword drawn, his horse's hooves pawing the air, its neck arched as if it had just been struck in the nose by a musket ball, or whatever the enemy fired at San Juan Hill. The city fathers were once at the point of removing the statue at the insistence of a tourist, something of an equestrian expert, if not a sculptor, but they hesitated at the last moment for two reasons; one, what do you do with a four-ton statue when you have removed it? and two, about forty flesh-and-blood horsemen rode in from the country in the style best reminiscent of a time a hundred years previous when city fathers were allowed to survive at all only by luck. Given time, the tourists' children would pull the whole thing down around their heads anyway.

Jolly passed along the final lane of the plaza, the one that received the most generous share of the afternoon sun. On the benches in two's and three's sat all the old men of the town who gathered there (from where, no one knew exactly) each Sunday to watch the town. They hushed their talk as Jolly walked by and only tapped their canes, impatient for him to be gone. He pulled out his cigarette pack and after choosing one let the package drop, as if by accident, onto the sidewalk between the two rows of benches.

"They'll fight like hell over those," he chuckled. He stepped from the curb to cross over to Doogle's.

"Did you want something?" the straggle-haired girl asked in a tone that said "You have a nerve."

"I did and I still do. A Coke and some cigarettes. Luckies."

"You get the weeds over yonder," she said, dipping a glass in the ice bin.

At the over-yonder counter Mr. Doogle himself presided, nervous and gold rimmed. His fidgets were constant, as if he feared some government inspector was about to bring the sky crashing down for selling cigarettes, beer, and prophylactics to minors.

"Luckies," said Jolly.

"You eighteen, young man?"

"Of course. Would I ask, otherwise?"

"Well, it pays to be safe. Cain't never tell about you young hoodlums. Seems to me, tho' I might be wrong, that eighteen gets younger about ever' year. Here y'are. That'll be twenty-four cents."

Before he finished his Coke, Jolly swung from the stool, and balancing an ash tray, the Coke and his cigarettes, he encased himself in the phone booth. Once settled, he considered the probability of getting through to Luke. It wasn't likely there was anything he'd care to hear Luke's mother say. He decided on the code ring.

"Number please," said the metallic voice.

"129, please." He waited until he heard the number ring once, then hung up. He watched the clock above the door of the drugstore until the red second hand had swept around twice.

"Number please."

"129, please."

"I'll ring again."

This time Luke answered promptly. "Jolly?" he said.

"Yeh. How are things on death row?"

"Sweet Jesus, was my old lady mad. She's been raising hell since three this morning. She finally taken a pill and went to bed."

"Can you get out?"

"Not a chance. She won't sleep forever."

"Did you see what I saw in church this morning?" Jolly asked and hoped he hadn't.

"No. Something?"

"I'll say. They're new. And is she ever! About five feet five, blond, and everything."

"How'd I miss that? What about the other, ah, features?" If it is possible to drool over the Bell System, Luke was.

"They're all in place. I know her last name, but how am I going to find out where she lives?"

Luke laughed. "She got a phone?"

"How the hell should I know? They're new, I told you."

"Look, moron. You ever thought of asking the operator do they have a phone?"

Jolly said, "That's an idea." And then he said, "Say, Ass-Hole Buddy, since you can't get out, how about me borrowing the Goose?"

"Sure. I'll go down the back stairs and leave the keys in it. Rather, I'll wait in the garage for you. I'd like to hear more about this."

"OK. Wish me luck," said Jolly and hung up. He deposited another dime and dialed O.

"Operator," said a voice, identical in nasal tone with the first.

"You got a number for Van Dearen? That's D-e-a-r-e-n." He listened while the operator rustled pages.

"Is that on Paseo Redondo?"

"Yes, ma'am," Jolly said, noting that that address would mean the Mountain Knolls area, something he hadn't anticipated.

"That number is 4112," said the voice.

Jolly waited for his dime to return and studied the bottom of his Coke glass, possibly in hopes there would be emblazoned the words he would use if he called 4112—and if 4112 answered.

He decided against the phone call and opened the booth. "Here you are, girl of my dreams," he said, setting his glass and the dime on the counter a dozen feet from where he had first sat. The waitress pushed a tired lock of hair back from her eyes and slid off the ice cream cabinet. Now she would have two wet circles to wipe off the counter.

Jolly approached Luke's from the alley and found him leaning against the back of the row of garages.

"Hey."

"Hey. Well?" Luke wore his quizzical expression.

"Well?" Jolly mocked. "I didn't call her."

"She have a phone?"

"Yes."

"You some kind of a nut? Whyn't you call her, chicken?"

"I found out her address—sort of. I think I'll just drive out that way and look around," Jolly said. Then he added, "Mountain Knolls."

"Mountain Knolls! Jeez, you can pick 'em. I bet

there's a law against cars as old as the Goose up there."

Jolly laughed. "Probably. You got the keys?"

Luke hesitated. "Yeh, I got 'em. But I don't know if I oughta let you go without your old dad. Think you can handle things?"

"What's there to handle in the middle of the goddam afternoon?" Jolly took the keys Luke handed him. He inspected the Blue Goose critically. "When in hell did you wash it last?"

"Well, Your Royal Patookus, I didn't know it was gonna mix with no damn Cadillacs or I'd a washed it. Jeez."

Jolly backed the coupe from the garage and then drove into the alley. Luke called, "You know what I always say; when in doubt—"

"Whip it out," Jolly finished, and the Blue Goose clattered down the alley.

TEN

JOLLY shifted into second gear as he drove through the flagstone pillars, and the car pointed up the first short hill. Mountain Knolls was not really in the mountains at all, but in the thick pine woods that edged the town on the south. The area was laced with small dirt roads that wound and circled and intercepted one another in what seemed an obvious (and well nigh successful) attempt to keep outsiders outsiders. The roads were unequalled for playing ditch 'em, to the immense displeasure of the residents, who had chosen country living partly in the belief that they would escape the wracking noises of the city only to find that the worst of the noises raced and honked and raised billows of dust before their very front doors every night. Many of the residents were only summer folks who could afford to escape the heat of the southern counties for a month or two during the year. The houses themselves, separated by several acres of unkempt natural pine growth, were studies in rustic architecture. One after the other vied for authenticity and number of screened porches. They were built only of native pine boards or logs and had unnecessarily steep roofs as if the snow could be expected to fall in greater quantities there.

Once over the first hill, Jolly divided his attention

between keeping the car on the road and peering for the proper wooden arrow that would designate Paseo Redondo. When he was at last on the right road he shifted his gaze to the houses, trying to choose the one most likely to conceal a girl who wore a white sailor hat.

Before long he recognized the sedan he had seen the Van Dearens drive that morning. It sunned itself in splotches of light and dark before the front steps of a house.

"Hey!" a voice yelled.

Jolly slammed on the brakes, and the small car slid to the edge of the curve, its bumper just resting against a high gray boulder. He heard a peal of laughter encircle the car. He looked atop the boulder.

There she was.

There she was sitting above him, laughing, her legs drawn up into her arms, her chin on her knees. Jolly wondered at their brownness. Her hair hung long and entirely straight on either side of her face. "Hi," she said.

"Hi," he said. There she was. He stepped out of the car. She watched him climb toward her. When he was part way there he stopped, his two hands leaning against the boulder.

"Good thing you yelled," he said.

Her laughter trembled. "Yes. You sure weren't looking at the road."

Jolly stepped up two more foot-holds. His eyes were level with hers as she lay the side of her face on her knees. There were yellow flecks among the brown of her eyes just the color of her skin below the white shorts she wore.

"Hi," he said, breathless not from the climb.

"You said that," she said. Jolly watched the bridge of her nose wrinkle when she laughed, stirring the freckles that paced across her cheeks. "My name is Dogie."

"Dogie? That's a calf." He waited a moment for her to explain. She did not. "I'm Jolly Osment," he said.

"Hi," she said and then, "Aren't you going to ask my last name?"

"I know that already."

She lifted her head, and most of her hair, the color of April laburnums, fell down her back. It was her turn to wait for an explanation.

"I asked," he said.

"Do you live here? In Cortez?"

"Yes," he said. "Have you come here in the summers before? I've never seen you." It was the truth, but he was seeing her now.

"No. Will I like it here?"

I will like you here, thought Jolly. He said, "I hope so. Where you from?"

"My dad has a ranch down near the border. This is the first summer he's been willing to leave it." She unclasped her knees and let her legs stretch down the face of the rock. She lay back on the flat surface. Her head lay on her hands. She watched Jolly's eyes, which had considerable trouble avoiding the space between her shirt and shorts where a band of brown skin showed. She began to twist a piece of her hair over a finger. She smiled.

Jolly turned his head on reluctant muscles and lifted his eyes beyond the brown thighs toward a clearing that formed a small valley just visible through the trees. "There's a nice little pond down yonder," he said. "With salamanders and frogs and all."

"OK," she said and sat forward. "Let's go see it." She gave him her hand to help her get down the granite face. At the bottom she said, "Are we going to drive, or what?"

"It's not far," he said, noticing she hadn't retrieved her hand and not wanting her to. "Let's walk."

"But I haven't any shoes." She looked to her feet.

"I'll fix that." Jolly thought wildly for a moment about the hand he still held. He let go of it, conscious of the difficulty of getting it back. He leaned one hand on the car and with the other slipped off his own shoes and socks and tossed them onto the front seat of the Blue Goose. "Now, we're even," he said.

She laughed. The freckles chased among the wrinkles across her face. "Crazy," was all she said and began walking.

"What do the kids do in Cortez in the summer?"

"Nothing much, I'm afraid. That is, nothing very exciting unless you use your imagination. Swim at the lake, mostly."

"Do you have wiener roasts? You know, around a fire at night—that sort of thing?"

"Oh, sure. We do that lots, too." He picked up a

pine cone and sent it over-ending toward a tree trunk. He missed.

"What are they like?"

"Just like wiener roasts anywhere, I guess." He saw that she was watching where she placed her feet at each step. "Why? Haven't you ever been on one?"

"No," she said.

He stopped short in the road. "What? You mean to tell me you never been on a wiener roast? Why the hell—the heck not?"

She faced him. The flecks in her eyes acted as lenses through which he could see the yellow of her hair. "I told you. I live on a ranch, thirty miles from the next one. And nothing in between but cactus and scrub oak and those darn cows."

"But—" said Jolly, perplexed.

"When school's on I ride twenty miles—twenty-three miles—each way to school on a bus. You can't exactly roast wieners on a school bus. Or do much of anything else." She began walking again. "I've always thought you had to have trees, lots of trees, for a wiener roast. Don't you?" she said.

He stepped beside her. "I don't know. I reckon so. I never went to any kind of thing—outdoors I mean—where there weren't trees."

"I never smelled anything as good as these pine trees. Do you like them?"

"Well, sure. I like them OK." He attempted a cautious sniff. They smelled dusty to him. "Haven't you ever seen trees before?"

She laughed. "Crazy," she said, "of course. But not like these, not pines, not by the hundreds."

Jolly didn't know precisely where to take the conversation next so he let it lie. It was enough to keep his mind from falling into pieces just being with this girl, let alone talk about trees.

"Don't you have any brothers or sisters? Or anybody to—to—"

"To play with?" she laughed. Then she didn't laugh. "No."

"Oh." The talk died again. Jolly fumbled in his shirt pocket for a cigarette, but after he had lured one from the pack he decided against using it. He put it back.

"There's the pond," he said, and she followed the direction of his finger. "Come on!" he yelled, and taking her hand he ran, pulling her mostly, down the last slope that dropped from the road and out of the pines into the clearing. The pond lay small and darker green than the grass, formed by a dam someone had once built for his own reasons in the ferny cleavage of a gully. The water wasn't very fresh most of the year; in fact, it came close to being stagnant. The cattails choked the edges all around except by the dam itself, standing straight or bending at angles (not curves) to dip their brown heads beneath the water. Two or three frogs plopped into the water without grace and surfaced again two feet away, their yellow legs hanging down, their eyes just above the water.

"Hey! Slow down," she yelled as he pulled her sliding, awkward, down the last grass. Her bare feet slipped from under her, and she finished second, on her behind, still holding Jolly's hand.

"What do you say, grace?" he said and fell to his knees beside her where the sound of her laughter fought between her words.

"Wow! I thought for a second we'd be swimming." She gathered up her knees in her arms. "It's a pretty pond," she said and tipped her face away from Jolly but not before he saw it pale. Her shoulders lifted with each breath.

"Yes. Course the water's not too fresh." He watched her back. "The frogs like it OK, I reckon." Through the material of her blouse stretched tightly across her back he could see her breath pumping in and out. "You OK?" he asked.

She hesitated a second and said "Yes." The sound carried out on one of the regular breaths. "Yes—I'm—OK—" She spaced the words with her breaths.

Then he heard the faint rasp like a small bellows makes when you spread the handles apart to draw in air. He suspended his own breath and listened. She lifted her head but kept it faced away. Beneath her hair long on her back, her shoulders continued to lift each time the bellows pumped in. Jolly stretched on his side and supported himself by one arm, bent at the elbow. He pulled a stem of turkey-foot grass. The outer tube slid up and off the inner stem smoothly. He twirled it back and forth between his thumb and fingers like the furious blades of a tiny helicopter. He put that stem between his teeth and pulled another. Then he rolled on his back and stared straight up at the sky, its blue more brilliant for the ragged edge of pine tops and the chalk clouds that rode high over one side. He listened for the rasps and counted the spaces between them until they grew farther and farther apart and then disappeared.

"Why didn't you tell me?" he asked.

She laughed shortly and turned toward him. The color had returned to her face except at the temples and around her lips. Those spots seemed translucent and faintly blue. "It's supposed to be better up here."

"Do you want to go back now?"

"No. Not yet," she said. She turned to the water. "It's a pretty pond," she said. She leaned to the side to reach a pine cone. Before she threw it she held it under her nose a moment. The frog complained shortly and ducked under the surface. His eyes and nose appeared again close by. Her laughter flounced brown and warm over the clearing.

"Jolly?" she said, and the word had never sounded that way.

"What?" he said. He rolled his head to watch the back of her hair three feet away.

"Nothing," she said. "You sound sleepy."

"I am. This kind of day makes me sleepy. Besides," he added, "I was kind of late getting in last night."

"Where you with a girl?"

"Yes," he said, which was only part of the truth. "Why?"

"No reason."

Jolly watched the clouds gathering white and round above the trees and listened to the feel of her near him.

He said to her, "Here, stretch out. The grass is soft."

She twisted toward him and saw where his hand patted the grass. Her eyes lifted to his and the gold flecks had disappeared. "No," she said and watched him.

"Why not? If you would you'd probably feel better."

"I feel all right." She watched his eyes as if she could read something there.

"What's the matter?" he asked.

"You want to make love to me, don't you," she said simply.

Jolly sat up. "What! No! Yes. I mean—why'd you say that?"

"Isn't that what you meant? When you asked me to lie down beside you?" Her eyes were wide and followed his wherever they turned. "Isn't that what you had in mind?"

To say it wasn't in his mind would be wrong, but it was far back, dark on the edges of his mind, just skirting there—not for a sunny afternoon in a pine clearing within the first hour of meeting.

"No! I didn't mean *that,*" Jolly said. He stood up. Her eyes followed him. He faced the pond and said, "I just meant it's a nice place to lie down and—and look at the sky. That's all."

After a moment she said, "Jolly?"

He turned to her. Her eyes still watched his but above them were creases of confusion. "Don't be angry. I'm sorry," she said and her eyes said "I don't understand."

He smiled. "You crazy. I'm not mad at you." The

lines passed from above her eyes and he said to himself "God knows I'm not mad at you, but I don't understand."

He walked out onto the little stone and cement dam to the middle and looked down into the water. All he saw was his own head, darkly, and the sky turned turquoise and pale green where the clouds were. He stretched one foot down until he could splash the front part of it in the water. He walked back across the dam.

"Dogie?" He had not called her by name before. "Does your mother like watercress?"

She was still watching him. "What is watercress?" she asked. "Is that some kind of fish or something?"

"No," he laughed and was relieved by it. "Come on, I'll show you." He did not reach for her hand but began walking down the stream bank where the water flowed after it left the dam. He could feel her follow behind him. After a short way he stopped and pointed. "There's some," he said and stepped down the bank to the stream.

"Those weeds?"

"These aren't weeds." He began pulling up small bunches of the yellow-green plants. "Here's some mint, too. How about some mint?" He added the darker, rough leaves to the bunches in his hand.

"Are you sure these aren't weeds?" and her laugh tilted a moment before falling down to the stream.

Jolly climbed up the bank. "Of course I'm sure. I bet your mother will like them. I bet she's had them before." He saw the gold flecks had returned to where they belonged. "Here, smell this." He crushed a leaf of mint and held it under her nose. She held his hand steady with her own.

"Hm. That's perfect. Wait—may I keep it?"

"Sure. You can have all you want."

"This is all I want," she said. "Shall we go?" She faced upward toward the road, then bent her face to the mint again, and a faint breath shuddered across her shoulders.

Beside the Blue Goose they stopped. "Thanks for the walk," she said, "and the mint."

"Oh. Here. Take all this to your mother." She reached her fingers above his hand to grasp the plants. "And Dogie?"

"Yes?"

"I'll—I'd like to take you on a wiener roast or something. OK?"

Her nose wrinkled and scattered the freckles. "Thank you, Jolly. I'd love it. When?"

"How about tonight?"

"No, not tonight. How about Tuesday? That is, if you don't have school work to do?"

Jolly grinned. "School can go—schoolwork can wait. I'll call you."

"All right." She turned to the path that curved up to her house. "Goodbye."

"So long," he said. He watched her walk away, her face bent to the bouquet of water plants in her hands. "So long," he said.

When the Blue Goose passed out through the flagstone pillars Jolly turned it to the west, away from town. "I'll just drive up the ridge and look. It's only four or five miles. And Luke's not going anywhere that he'll need the car."

The road climbed gently until the end of the Mountain Knolls area where the pavement stopped. From there the climb was steeper but not too much for any car, including Luke's. The road rocked down into dips every few hundred feet. Those would be rushing, mad little streams when the rains broke. Birch trees grew spotted black and white on the edges of the road where the dips crossed, their trunks rummaging among the wild ferns that loved their shade. Above them, thicker and taller as the road climbed, grew the giant ponderosas, dusty with age and thirst.

The road made its way along the outer ridges encircling Castle Dome, a barren shaft of black granite that rose immense and lonely above the pines and manzanita. You could see the Dome from town, but once on the road to it, it was hidden until you found yourself at its foot with nothing but forty miles of fast-falling cliffs and slopes, brush-covered, that stretched to the next range of mountains on the west. It was to this view of the valley that Jolly drove.

Today the far mountains were bluer and less purple than they would be after the rains had washed the air and crisscrossed the slopes with new gullies.

Jolly walked to the edge of the drop and looked down three thousand feet and across twenty miles. If the air were clear he could have picked out a speck of white, or the wink of glass that would be a house or perhaps the general store. He grasped the sleek red limb of a manzanita and, using it for a balance, slid three or four feet down the slope to a flat rock that jutted out from the earth. From there, there was nothing to see but miles and miles of the country he had once roamed with Jamie, or more often with Pekoe, the dog. There, overlooking the ragged terrain that once hid bands of renegades and Indians whose bones gave the valley its name, nothing intercepted the view but visions of April laburnum playing along the top of the haze that hung like remembrance against the far mountains.

He should have asked Jamie where he was staying. Not that he would have found out. But if he knew, he'd barge in and ask him. Probably shacked up somewhere with a woman. He'd barge in anyway. Let him alone, like hell. There was just one question he wanted to ask Jamie, and he could damn well stop whatever he was so busy doing long enough to answer it.

ELEVEN

JAMIE LAUGHED. "Hell, no, Mandy, you can't fall in love with somebody in one hour or one day."

She raised herself on her elbow and pushed the hair back from his forehead. "But I did, so what do you think of that?"

"No, you didn't. Just because of the kid, and the thinking about it so long."

She flopped on her pillow and pulled up on the sheet. "Well, two years ought to be enough, don't you think? And darn long ones."

Jamie held the baby on his knees bent up under the sheet. The boy laughed every time he heard either of their voices. He held one finger on each of Jamie's hands and bounced on his fat, wet bottom. "Look, you haven't—we haven't even seen each other a dozen times. And are you going to change him? I got up and got him, you know."

"Don't change the subject, that's what don't change. So you don't think I'm in love, Mr. Big? Well, let me demonstrate."

"Hey! Stop it," Jamie squirmed, his hands occupied with holding the child. "You'll make me drop the kid. Stop that!" The child laughed aloud when he toppled off Jamie's knees between them. "See? There," he lifted the boy and set him astride his mother's chest. "You want something to hold, how's that present?"

"God, he's drowned." She set him off the edge of the bed onto the floor. "Now, just look. I'm sopping."

"I'm looking, I'm looking," Jamie laughed.

She stopped rubbing and reached for his face. She pulled it down close to hers and watched the blue eyes laughing. "I think if I can just keep you around long enough this time—"

"That's what I'm afraid of. Ow! You're pulling my ears out by the roots, you know."

She pulled harder, then relaxed her hold and linked her fingers behind his neck. "You're beautiful," she said.

He laughed, but gently. "That's the first time anybody ever said that. My mother always said I was the ugliest little kid ever born, and I don't think that opinion's changed much."

"No, you're not." She pulled his head down closer. "Well, are you going to, or not."

"I'm thinking about it."

"Maybe you ought to bring along that cute brother of yours so you could get some rest. What's his name?"

"Jolly. But he isn't."

"Isn't what?"

"Jolly. They ought to have named him Morry, or something. Short for Morose."

"Well, you'll have to do." She twisted his hair around her fingers. "Weren't you ever in love, Jamie? I mean, really. With somebody?"

He arched back his head, and with his one free hand

unclasped her fingers. He swung his legs off the opposite side of the bed and sat with his back toward her. "Goddamit, Mandy. Don't start again. No, I told you. No."

She watched silently as he rose and scooped his clothes from the chair and stomped naked across the floor into the bathroom. "OK, sourpuss," she said to herself. She turned over on her stomach. She stretched out one arm toward the child, who sat where she had placed him on the floor, now trying to fit one of Jamie's boots over his head. She hung her head upside down over the edge of the bed and lifted up the boot. "You see?" The child howled in delight. "I told you. You wait and see." She yanked the boot down over his eyes again.

From the back of the chair she took Jamie's big robe and wrapped it around her and searched to one side and then the other for the ends of the belt. "I'll make you a deal," she said aloud.

"What?" came Jamie's voice from the bathroom.

"I said—" The door opened a foot.

"What'd you say?"

"I said," she lowered her voice, "I'll make you a deal."

"The hell you will. This morning you don't get out of it."

"But I can make better eggs than you can."

"Well, I don't care. He's yours—"

"And yours."

"—and it's your turn to change him. I'd rather eat

my cooking. Anyway, your coffee won't take any prizes at any fair I ever heard of."

"And I suppose you've seen 'em all." She pushed the bathroom door open with her foot and leaned one hip against the jamb. The door hit Jamie on the back. "Don't cut your throat."

"Someday you're going to ram that doorknob so far up my—"

"Ah, ah." She wagged a finger.

He turned from the mirror, his face lathered except for a wide streak down one cheek. "You want something, nosey? You know this bathroom's about big enough for a midget. I don't see how you get all that," he dabbed the safety razor toward her body "in here —not and close the door."

"You'd have more room in here yourself in the mornings if you could stand closer to the sink," she giggled.

He wiped a great gob of shaving cream from his face and flung it at her. "Get out of here!" She pulled the door closed fast enough so that most of the cream splattered against it on the inside.

Mandy jiggled the coffee pot and lifted the lid. She held it under the faucet and let water run slowly down through the percolator holes over the old grounds. She set it on the three-burner gas plate and lit a fire.

"OK, drowned rat," she said. She swooped the boy from the floor and held him high, at arm's length. "Let's see what can be done about your condition."

The baby laughed, and his blue eyes became only dark slits above his fat cheeks.

TWELVE

ON TUESDAY evening, Jolly sat in the downstairs office of the Meaders Mortuary awaiting Luke, whose ablutions even for a wiener roast were painstaking and slow. Jolly thumbed backwards through old issues of *The Saturday Evening Post* and watched George Meaders studying a huge chart on his desk.

"It'll rain, you know," said Mr. Meaders to the chart. "I know," said Jolly. He traded the magazine for another, turned it over and started from the back. "It always does at a picnic or anything."

Mr. Meaders refolded part of the chart and opened a different square. "Where you boys going?"

"Badger Creek, I guess. I don't know."

The sun just setting in the clouds threw across the room that peculiar bright light that comes only before a rain. It was brighter yet less colorful than the ordinary setting sun. George Meaders swung his chair so that his back was to the window, then held up the chart, browned along each crease from years of folding and unfolding.

"What's that?" asked Jolly.

"This? It's a map of the cemetery. Look." Jolly stood and walked to the desk behind Mr. Meaders' chair. "See these little boxes?"

"Are those the graves?"

"Yes."

"Are those the names of the people buried in them?" He leaned closer over Mr. Meaders' shoulder. "Do you have the names of all the people buried out there?"

"Yep. See there? There's the mausoleum."

The mausoleum looked surprisingly insignificant on paper. Just a larger square with four rows of names printed in tiny close letters. Jolly's glance circled around the larger square. "Which way is west?" he asked.

"Here." Jolly followed Mr. Meaders' finger, but a fold in the chart obstructed the squares close to the mausoleum. "These blank places are plots that haven't been sold yet. And these blue numbers tell us in the cross file if the plot is owned but not occupied," Mr. Meaders chuckled.

They heard Luke clattering down the stairs from above. Jolly watched as Mr. Meaders refolded the chart.

"Well, patookus, you ready?" Luke came into the office. Despite his lengthy preparations he wore faded Levis over which his shirttail flapped in back, and his hair hung straight to one side of his forehead.

"I been ready for half my life." Jolly saw Mr. Meaders place the chart in a wooden filing cabinet, slide it shut and lock it. Then he locked the other filing drawers and his desk.

"I'd advise you two to get home at a reasonable hour," said Mr. Meaders. "Your mother won't take kindly to another all-night spree,'' he said to Luke.

''We'll be *in* early,'' Luke winked to Jolly, ''and we should be home not long after.''

''Get the hell outa here,'' said George Meaders.

''Dad? Can we use the big car?'' Luke asked.

''What's the matter with yours now?'' He rubbed the sides of his nose at the bridge with his thumb and fingers, under his glasses.

''Nothing's the matter with it,'' said Luke. ''It's just crowded, you know, with four people and all.'' He knew his father would make only a token objection.

''All right,'' sighed Mr. Meaders. ''Only we've got a funeral in the morning. I want that car washed before ten, you hear?''

''Yes, sir,'' said Luke, and the two boys scrambled out the back door toward the garages.

''Where?'' asked Luke. The black car dipped from the alley onto the street.

''The girls,'' said Jolly. ''Dogie got all the wieners and crap.''

''Dogie. With a name like that she must be something,'' Luke said.

Jolly smiled. ''She is.'' And then he repeated, ''She is.''

''This I gotta see.''

''You can *see* all you want. Just keep your goddam meat hooks to yourself.''

''I promise. At least tonight,'' Luke laughed. ''I expect to have my hands very full tonight.''

''Yeh, Babe Wooten. Couldn't you find anybody

else? She and Dogie are about as much alike as two *snow*flakes, for chrissake.''

''Boy, I keep tellin' ya. You gotta keep the fire warm.''

''But a wiener roast! Babe's not quite the type, you know.'' Jolly pointed to the stone-pillared entrance to Mountain Knolls.

Luke laughed. ''I'm only interested in roasting one certain wienie tonight.'' The car shifted to a lower gear and began to climb the first hill. The scent of the air changed perceptibly as the road delved among the close-standing pines. The air was sharper and carried a stronger hint of rain. To the right the trees stood darker, their green turned gray against patches of the orange sky.

''Beautiful sunset,'' said Jolly, thinking that she would be seeing it and exclaiming it, too.

''Yeh. Where the hell do I go now?'' asked Luke. He stopped the car at a point where three roads diverged on their own and wound out of sight.

Jolly brought his attention back to the roads. ''There,'' he said, pointing. ''It's not far now.'' He leaned forward in the seat, his forearm on the dash, and watched for the house. He hadn't remembered that it took so long to get there from the main road. ''There!'' he said. ''There it is.''

''Jeez. How the hell you get up that driveway?'' Luke asked, but he turned the car toward the house anyway, and as the front rose sharply he stepped hard on the accelerator and the big car spun its wheels and lifted deep-throated up to the flat place before the house.

There she was.

Before they had opened the car doors there she was coming down the steps, her arms encircling a huge cardboard box, her face partly hidden by it. Her laughter came before her.

Jolly reached her at the bottom of the steps and took the box. "I thought you'd never get here," she said, and he was startled to see that she hadn't changed in two days. The gold flecks in her eyes still almost matched her hair, but a shade darker, and the freckles still moved when she laughed.

He wanted to say "I'd have been here a thousand hours ago if I had my way." He said, "What the heck you got in this box? It weighs about a ton."

Her laughter, which sort of hung around on the edges all the time, came back into focus. "Just all the things you said to get," she said. "Are you Luke?" she asked, turning to him.

"Oh. Sorry. Luke, this is Dogie," said Jolly. He glanced at Luke's face. What he saw there both pleased him (Luke liked her) and displeased him (Luke liked her).

"Hi," she said.

"Hello," said Luke. Jolly controlled a quick angry impulse to comment on Luke's sappy face. Instead he plunked the box into Luke's arms.

"Here," he said. And to her he said, "You ready? You better wear a jacket or something. It'll get cold if it rains."

"OK. I have to tell Mother I'm leaving." She ran back up the steps and slammed the screen door.

Jolly heard a low whistle behind him. He turned. Luke leaned against the car, still holding the cardboard box. "Jesus Christ," he spoke reverently.

"Well?" said Jolly.

"Not bad. Not bad at all," grinned Luke. "You wanta drive?"

"Hell, no, I don't want to drive. If you're driving you got at least one hand occupied."

"What a way to treat an old buddy," sighed Luke and turned to open the back door of the car. He placed the box on the floor and shut the door. He reached one hand into his pants pocket and held it with the other hand while he drew out a nickel. "I'll flip you."

Jolly extended the middle finger of his right hand. "Screw you, friend," he said. "And no trades."

"But Babe's a sure thing," insisted Luke, good-natured but willing to be serious.

"Yeh? I thought you said after she'd had your fancy equipment she'd be ruined for anybody else." The screen door slammed. "Knock it off, now, for crapssake."

"We're off!" she said. Jolly stepped forward and took her hand deliberately and led her to the back door of the car. "We'll swing by for Luke's girl and then we're ready," he said.

Dogie stopped briefly. "Gee. This is the biggest car I ever saw. You going to ride all alone up there, Luke?" she asked and stepped into the car.

"Looks like," said Luke, sliding into the front seat. "Temporarily."

While Luke backed the car around and got it headed down the steep driveway, Jolly planned what subtle moves it would take to get his arm around her shoulders or her hand in his. Before he braved either she clasped his wrist with her hand lying in his. She would always surprise him, he decided; in fact, she was a surprise.

An hour later Luke stopped the car beside one of the cleared camping areas at Badger Creek. In front the headlights shone across a low stone grill and a Forest Service garbage can, pushing the new darkness back over the little silent stream that darted black and silver.

"This OK?" asked Luke, disengaging his arm and lifting it, crooked, from over Babe's shoulders. Her head rose into full view in the light. "Cripes. This is really out in the boon-docks, ain't it," she said and stretched.

"It's wonderful," said Dogie, peering in all directions as if to pierce the dark. Jolly felt a wave of excitement pass from her hand to his.

"Fine," said Jolly. "Let's get with it." He opened his door and reached to lift out the cardboard box. "We have to get a fire going first. Hey, you two," he addressed the front seat, "knock it off. If you want to do something, gather firewood."

Babe and Luke giggled from the front seat and separated. "You guys got any beer?" she asked. Jolly left Luke to smooth over that one and led the way to the stone grill. Dogie walked beside him, if you could call that walking. She very nearly skipped.

"It's *per*fect," she said. "Where do you get the wood?"

"We're in a forest, crazy," said Jolly.

"Can you build a fire?"

"Sure. But, before you ask, not by rubbing two sticks together."

She laughed and it dimmed the artificial light. "Weren't you a Boy Scout?" she said.

"Not a very high-grade one. I never could see why you had to rub *sticks* together when you could buy enough matches for a dime to burn down the whole damn forest. Excuse me." He set the box beside the fireplace.

"You wouldn't make a very good Indian," she said.

"So who wants to be an Indian?" He took her hand and they walked toward the trees where there would be dry limbs and pine needles for the fire.

"Yes," she pursued the topic, "but how would you keep warm if you *were* an Indian?"

"Just like the rest of them around here. Wine." He picked up a small limb and used it like a cane. "Or I would get my squaw to whip me up a blanket on her spinning wheel."

"Loom."

"What?"

"Loom. You make blankets on a loom," she said. Then she said, "I think."

He laughed. "OK. Here, make yourself useful." He handed her two small limbs. "At this rate it'll be midnight before we get a fire going."

She followed behind him holding out her arms to

cradle the sticks he handed her. "It's getting pretty dark in here, isn't it?" she said, her eyes searching among the pines.

"Afraid of Indians?" he said. He walked on, bending now and then to collect firewood. "You're more apt to find a coyote or a bobcat than an Indian. Or a polecat."

"Jolly?"

He turned at the timid sound of her voice. He couldn't see her face, but her head was silhouetted against the car's faint lights. He walked the few steps back to her. "Crazy, don't be afraid," he said and touched her shoulder. "We'll go back now." As they walked he watched her face emerge like morning in the growing light and her mouth began to smile again.

When the fire was going well Luke switched off the headlights and he and Babe walked to the fire carrying blankets. "Big Chief got-um fire going," stated Luke.

Jolly thought that from all appearances his wasn't the only fire going. He saw Luke surreptitiously adjust himself behind the folded blanket on his arm. "Get some sticks to roast with," Jolly said.

Babe tossed her blanket on the ground and sat on it, watching the fire. She turned to Dogie. "I coulda sure used a beer. How about you?" She yanked on the bottom of the sweat shirt that appeared to be her only upper garment.

"Well," began Dogie, "I guess—well, I guess we just forgot it." She looked to Jolly.

"We got Cokes, Babe. That'll have to do. Here, you two can spread out these things on that blanket and open the jars and all. As soon as Ponce de Leon gets back with the sticks we're in business."

Luke meandered back into the light, whittling a point on a green stick. He carried another under his arm.

"Don't you ever *hurry?*" Babe called. "God, my stomach's actually talking, I'm so hungry." She unscrewed the lid of a jar and drew out a fat dill pickle. She held it between her teeth while she closed the lid.

"Keep your shirt on," said Luke, exchanging the stick in his hand for the one under his arm which he then began to strip and whittle.

"I intend to," said Babe, chewing the pickle. "Gimme that stick you got finished." She pierced three wieners with the stick and held them over the flames.

"Hold them down there near the coals," said Jolly. "You'll burn the hell—the heck out of them up there."

"Don't tell me about wienies," she said, and Luke howled. But she lowered them out of the high flames.

"Let me roast some," said Dogie. She took the other stick from Luke and pierced two wieners as Babe had. Her nose wrinkled from the heat of the fire and she held her head back and to one side. "Is this right?" she asked.

Jolly watched her smile at the fire and watched as Luke bent over her and with his hand on hers readjusted the position of the roasting stick an inch. Luke seemed to notice, too, the flames reflect in her hair and brighten the gold in her eyes as she raised her face to smile at him.

"God damn!" said Babe as she drew her wieners from the fire. "Don't them look good."

Later, after Babe's gastronomical appetite was satisfied, and the fire had died to occasional pops and glows, Jolly sat with Dogie on one of the blankets, leaning against the furrowed brown trunk of a pine. He chatted foolishly about the forest, the town, the rain that still threatened—anything to keep her face turned toward his and away from Luke and Babe who lay on their blanket on the other side of the fire, their low-whispered talk interrupted only by Babe's chuckles and periods of silence.

"Jolly," Dogie said, stopping his flow of talk. "When are you going to kiss me?" Her eyes, wide and serious, watched his.

How do you figure a girl like this? Jolly opened his mouth and closed it, dumbly, like the goldfish in the plaza pond. He laughed shortly. This was the first time a girl had had to ask.

"I guess I do talk too much," he said. "How about right now?" He bent to kiss her and felt her lips soft and immobile, inexperienced. He moved his lips experimentally against hers, and they remained soft, yet she did not pull back, and her eyes watched his, curiously.

"Thank you," she said when he stopped.

He moved his arm farther down her shoulder and reached across the front of her waist and pulled her toward him and met her lips again. She moved to him easily but remained relaxed, unresponsive. Jolly drew back his head and studied her face. The gold flecks had brightened, if anything. She seemed to wait for his next move, to be told what she should do. Jolly rejected the exploratory thought that passed through his mind.

"Why are you smiling?"

The idea was ridiculous.

"No reason," he said.

Not with this girl. Not with Dogie.

"Where are they going?"

Luke and Babe had picked up their blanket and were walking toward the car, she reaching back to tug at the band of her sweat shirt, he pulling down on his Levis pockets to ease the tightness that had ridden too high. At the car he held the rear door for her to enter then closed it after them.

"What are they going to do?"

Jolly thought, if you only knew. He said to her that Luke and Babe were probably tired of the lumpy ground or were cold or something. To change the subject he withdrew his arm from her shoulders and leaned forward on his knees to pitch more wood on the fire. He remained to watch the flames climb quickly over the dry pine wood, brightening the night as they cracked.

"I like a pine fire," he said.

"What?"

He turned to her. "I said I like a pine fire. Don't you?"

She watched him come back to her. "Yes," she said. "Yes." She leaned forward a few inches so his arm could encircle her shoulders again. Instead, he asked her if she wouldn't like a pickle or a toasted marshmallow. A frown passed her face and she smiled. "OK," she said and leaned back against the tree.

"OK which?"

"A toasted pickle," she said, and her laugh stilled the night insects' songs.

Jolly was relieved by her laugh and the orange light that mazurkaed in her hair. "Crazy," he said.

All right, maybe. Jolly moved back from the fire again. Dogie's eyes watched his even as he knelt and took her face in his two hands, pressing the orange light against her skin. Her lips began to mimic each inquest of his. Because her eyes still watched his, he moved his face so that it rested beside hers, by her neck. Whenever his arms pressured her she moved forward to him. He felt her back stiffen and shiver when his hand stopped over one breast, but because she did not remove it, the hand went on to the buttons of her blue plaid shirt.

It was then the storm broke. As happens in the high pine forests, it came with the first lightning as if someone had ripped a huge water-filled balloon and sent its contents down on everything thirsty below.

"No," Jolly whispered and clenched Dogie to him, trying to wrap his whole self over her as if by shielding her from the rain it would see and cease.

The little fire hissed and sent up spurts of white smoke, but it was no match for the downpour and was extinguished by the time Jolly and Dogie—she shrieking, delighted—had gathered the blanket and box of food.

"We better get to the car!" he yelled, louder than was necessary for her to hear. He guided her to the front door and opened it, but not before they were drenched. "Quick!" His voice was urgent. He threw the box across the front seat and shoved her in. The inside lights of the car flared brightly.

Dogie stopped, one knee on the seat, the other foot on the ground. She stared into the back seat. "God," thought Jolly. "Jesus God. They could've at least used the blanket." He pushed against Dogie's bottom and shoulder and sent her sprawling across the cardboard box on the other side of the seat. He slammed the door and waited.

"What the hell's going on?" Luke said. He was plainly angry.

"It's raining, idiot," said Jolly. "We better get the hell outa here before the mud's ass-deep." Well, he wasn't inclined right then to be cautious. He felt for the key in the ignition, found it, and started the engine. He raced it a few seconds before turning on the headlights. He put the car in reverse and leaned over the seat in order to back up onto the road. He tried to ignore the rearrangements being made in the back seat, now only faintly visible in the reflected light, and concentrated on backing the car.

Once on the road, he shifted to forward gear, and his eyes passed over Dogie. She sat low in the seat, looking straight ahead, her arms crossed over each other tightly. Jolly gave the road more attention than it needed and drove too fast so that the back of the car slewed on the curves.

"Take it easy, Joll," Luke spoke calmly. "Take it easy."

On the paved road Jolly relaxed some and lighted a cigarette. The cigarette was reason not to talk. Outside, the white streaks of lightning cracked over the forest, lighting the asphalt channel over which the car traveled and the border of trees that seemed to stretch upwards in delight toward the rain.

Jolly felt Dogie edge toward him, her arms still clasped about her body. "You scared?" he said and smiled down on her head. She moved the rest of the way to him and seemed to welcome his arm.

"A little," she said. "I've never seen anything like it. The storm, I mean."

He ignored the unnecessary added explanation and said, "We'll have these sudden storms off and on all summer. They're loud—"

"—and wet."

"Yes, but they only last a little while. It'll be over by the time we get home."

"We're going home?" she asked.

"Yes," he answered. "We're going home."

No one spoke more than to comment on the conditions of the weather until Jolly stopped the car on the road at the bottom of Dogie's driveway. "We'll have to walk," he said. "The driveway'll be too muddy."

"OK," she said and waited for him to open the door. Without looking toward them she called goodnight to Luke and Babe and stepped onto the road.

"Here. Take some of this stuff," said Jolly.

"No. You keep it," she said.

"What'll I do with all this? You take it. Your mother—"

"I don't want any of it!" she interrupted. She turned to walk away. Jolly ran to catch her hand. They slipped in the mud, and he pulled her up the driveway quickly because the rain had not stopped.

On her porch she faced him and said, "Goodnight, Jolly. I loved it."

"Wait a minute, Dogie." He reached his hand to brush back a strand of wet yellow hair from her face. She took his hand from her face and held it. Her eyes watched his in the light from the windows. He smiled and that seemed to be enough for her. He put his arms around her, but she averted his face in favor of his shoulder.

"Jolly?"

"Yes."

"Jolly, they were making love, weren't they?" she said.

He took longer to answer than is needed to say yes or no. He felt her back heave beneath his hands. He should not have pulled her up the steep muddy driveway so fast, he remembered. "I shouldn't have pulled you so fast," he said.

She said, "It doesn't matter." The bellows sound had started. She lifted her head. Her face wore a question. She waited.

He pushed her head back on his shoulder and said, "Yes."

In a few minutes her breath came more naturally. She moved back from him and smiled, but the freckles didn't chase across her face. "Goodnight, Jolly," she said and opened the door of her house.

THIRTEEN

THE following morning Jolly awoke late and lay in bed even later. His last exam at school was not until the next day so there was very little he had to do better than stare at the low ceiling and wonder about the strange yellow-haired girl whom he had seen but twice —three times counting the morning in church. His mother had no objections to his lying late abed, because he had come in early the night before. He heard her puttering quietly about the house fulfilling her part of a tacit agreement that had always seemed backwards to him. At ten-thirty, no longer able to forestall a trip to the bathroom, he swung his legs off the bed and jammed them into his Levis.

Later he studied some, but *Silas Marner* yellowed like the old miser's gold before his eyes, and the words came alive like freckles moving. He rejected the desire to phone, because you weren't supposed to phone girls, that is, special girls, before noon.

He closed the book. "Mom. I think I'll go down to school for a while."

His mother came to the kitchen door, wiping flour from her hands on a cloth. "You have a test today?"

"No, but I need to clean out my locker and stuff." He tied his shoelaces, sitting on the living room sofa.

"What about lunch? You need to eat some lunch."

"I'll eat somewhere, Mom. Don't worry."

"Lord a mercy, the kind a food you eat. I don't know *when* you've had a square meal. Sometimes you don't eat enough to shake a stick at. You'll dry up and blow away." She followed him into the bathroom and stood watching him comb his hair.

"OK, Mom, OK. I'm not exactly skin and bones."

"You put too much water on your hair. It'll all fall out someday, doing that. You ought to brush it."

"Like Jamie, you mean? As I remember he brushed his, and it still fell out."

His mother turned momentarily to view a pot of something on the stove. "Jamie's hair is different. He has his father's hair."

"OK, Mother. Excuse me." He moved past her, through the kitchen toward the bedroom. She followed.

"How was your picnic last night? You never said."

"It was OK." He took a shirt from his closet.

"You-all came home mighty early. Why'd you decide to come home so early? Didn't you and her get along?"

"Mother," he said, "don't *quiz* me. It rained. And everything was fine. OK?"

She drew up stiffly. "You needn't get on your high horse. You just never tell me anything. You could be dead and buried and I'd be the last to know. It's a come-off."

She withdrew to her pots and her pans, and Jolly buttoned his shirt, then stuffed his pockets with his change and wallet, his comb, and a clean handkerchief. "See you later," he called and closed the front door.

In her kitchen Mattawilde Osment clucked her tongue and wondered what would finally become of that boy.

At school Jolly walked first into the gymnasium locker rooms and was greeted by the dirty socks-n'-jocks odor that had permeated the walls for so long that it never subsided, not even in the summer when the school was closed for three months. He took the lock off the handle, knowing he would never remember the combination by fall. His gym clothes he rolled in the stiff towel as neatly as possible and tied the laces of his tennis shoes together for easier carrying.

"Fingers!" A door slammed and big Guppy's voice reverberated against the metal lockers and echoed through the tiled showers he loved so well. "How the hell?" he said.

"Hi, Guppy." Jolly shut the door of his locker and turned. "You still around? I thought you'd be long gone by now."

Guppy threw his meaty body down prone on a wooden bench. "Shit," he said. "Coach called me and said I had ta clean out my friggin' locker."

Jolly opened his mouth to say something like "Me too," but Guppy, well started, continued his diatribe. "Christ, what a night," he said, flinging one huge arm over his eyes. "Me and the guys really laid one on."

"You get drunk?"

"Drunk? That ain't the *half* of it. I feel like a goddam punching bag or something. Jesus, I'll be glad to get outa this friggin' dump." He sat up suddenly. "You know what old lady Kastner gimme in English, fer chrissake?"

"She pass you?"

"She gimme a four. A goddam *four.*" Guppy shook his head. "I shoulda got better'n a goddam four, don't ya think? Christ, I taken that course three times."

Jolly laughed. "Guppy, you ought to be glad she passed you at all. She probably only did so she wouldn't have to see your ugly face again next year."

Guppy looked up at Jolly to better decide the nature of his comment. Satisfied, he studied his hands hanging limply between his knees. "Ah, screw her," he said and thus closed the subject.

"You're going to graduate tonight, aren't you?"

Guppy grinned. "You bet your sweet ass I am. Hey! You can't smoke in here! This is the *lock*er room, fer chrissake."

"I can't think of a better place."

"What if they catch you?" Guppy's face hung in honest concern.

"Maybe they'll bar me from this damn gym forever. That would be about the greatest injustice known to man."

"You're some kind of a nut," said Guppy. "Hey! Know what me and the guys'r gonna do tomorra night to celebrate?"

"No. What."

"We're gonna shagg ass to Nogie."

"Nogales?"

"Yeh, man! First I'm gonna get me about a dozen beers, and then I'm gonna plunk down my three dollars and get me the biggest, fattest, hottest piece a tail on

Canal Street." Guppy flopped back on the bench and yelped.

Jolly flicked the ash from his cigarette on the floor and spread it with his shoe. "Who's going with you?" he asked.

"Hell, I don't know. Burgess and Culp, I guess. And Skinny if his old lady'll let him outa her sight." He sat up again. "And then ya know what I'm gonna do, Fingers?"

"What."

"I'm gonna do it all over again!"

"You're going to break this goddam bench if you don't quit flopping on it. You ever been there before, Guppy?"

"Shit yes. Lotsa times." Guppy grinned his secret thoughts to the ceiling. "Ain't you?"

"No."

Guppy sat up again. "You ain't?"

"I said no," Jolly said.

Guppy watched Jolly's face closely. "You ain't?" he repeated quietly. "I bet you never even had a piece."

Jolly walked to the far end of the room before he answered. "Sure I have, dope. All the time." He dropped the cigarette into a toilet and with his foot on the handle watched it swirl away.

"Well, I got to go, Guppy," he said, gathering up his things.

"Say, Osment. Why the hell don't you go with us?"

Jolly smiled but said, "No thanks. Not this time. I—"

"We're gonna have a real blast."

"—I have a date."

"Stick around while I clean out my goddam locker."

"I can't, Guppy. I have to see the principal or somebody." He opened the door that led onto the basketball courts. "See you later, Hero."

"So long," said Guppy as he stretched out on the bench.

Jolly stopped by Mrs. Perley's room to see if she was in the mood to divulge final geometry grades. She wasn't, so he went on to his hall locker and faced the job of separating a nine months' collection of ill-related items into a keep pile, a sell-back-to-the-bookstore pile, and a throw-away pile.

At twelve he crossed the small campus to the phones in the hall opposite the office. "4112, please," he responded to the nasal voice. He listened as the phone rang twice.

"Hello?"

"Is Dogie there?"

"Who? Oh, Dorothy. Yes."

He heard the voice call Dogie to the phone.

"Yes?"

"Hi, Dogie."

"Hello, Jolly."

"What's the matter with your voice?"

"I caught cold last night, I'm afraid. It's not bad, though. Mother's not too happy about my going out tonight."

Jolly laughed. "You're getting pretty cocky, aren't you?" he said. "I don't believe I've got around to *ask*ing you yet."

"Asking me?" she said after a moment.

"Yeh. We could go to a movie or somewhere. I really ought to study for that test tomorrow, but in this case—"

"Jolly," she interrupted.

"What?"

"Jolly, I already have a date for tonight." Her voice came quietly over the phone. "Jolly?"

"You al*ready* have a date? But, Dogie, I thought—well, I thought—" He traced over the number 4112 with his pencil on the plywood panel that was nailed anew each fall on the wall by the students' telephone. "Never mind," he said. Then he said, "Who?"

"Who do I have a date with?"

"Yes."

He heard her cough dimly, as if her head were turned away from the phone. She said, "With Luke."

"Luke!" Jolly nearly shouted. "With *Luke?*"

"Yes."

"But why—but when—when did he—"

"He called me this morning. Jolly, you're not *mad*, are you? You sound mad."

The point of his pencil broke on the number 2. He stuffed the stub into his shirt pocket. Then he answered, "No, crazy. Why should I be mad?"

"Well," she laughed, "you just *sound*ed—"

"Look, Dogie," he said, "I have to go. I got some things to do. I'll call you tomorrow maybe. OK?"

"Well, OK. Jolly, listen, I didn't—"

"Bye, Dogie," he said and hung up the receiver. He leaned against the small counter that held the telephone and stared blankly at his tennis shoes lying crazily atop his notebook. "Son of a *bitch!*"

"Osment!"

Jolly turned. There stood Mr. Hanfield, coach-turned-counselor. Jolly flushed before the indignant stare.

"Whatya mean using that kinda language on the school grounds? Look, just because school is about out don't mean you can—"

"I'm sorry, Mr. Hanfield." Jolly picked up his tennis shoes and gym clothes and books. "I didn't know—I mean, I didn't mean—"

"Look," the man said, coming closer, "something the matter?" He peered at Jolly's face, then reached out a hand to Jolly's shoulder. "Look, if there's something—"

"Nothing's the matter," Jolly said and moved out from under the hand.

"You look kinda—well, you look like you been—"

"Please, Mr. Hanfield." Jolly turned to the glass door that led onto the parking lot. "I'm sorry. There's nothing the matter." He shoved hard with his hip on the metal bar that opened the door.

Mr. Hanfield rubbed one hand over his gray head and readjusted his glasses. "That boy's gonna be a real case about next year," he said. He watched Jolly's back as he walked across the lot. "That big and he don't like football or basketball or nothing." He wagged his head. "A real case."

Jolly climbed the steep path that ran over the hill behind the school to the low stone wall that embraced the Historical Museum, a series of dark, squat buildings in which were mercilessly guarded such things as stuffed owls from the homes of early persons of note in the territory, or rusted and rotted wagon wheels that had dropped off along the way as white men routed the Indians back to the sage brush and claimed the pine forests in the name of the Union. Jolly sat on the wall from where he could look down on the pink-topped school buildings, and beyond to the town itself—the plaza, Whiskey Row, the drugstore, the dimestore, Penney's—all settled down like an alley full of motley cats for a nap in the heat of the day.

Jolly wondered in passing which of the old widows that guarded the museum's priceless junk would recognize him sitting there and report the fact of his smoking to his mother. He followed the progress of a white-shirted figure across the school parking lot far below and tried to guess who it was. He saw the man enter a blue car and watched it back up, then move forward over the nearly empty lot and onto the street. Mr. Smithson; typing. He heard the horn of a diesel engine howl through the heat waves over the town from the railroad yards. He remembered the time when he was very small when he and Jamie got in trouble for putting pennies on the rails so that the coal-burning engines would flatten them into oval copper disks. He looked for recognizable animal shapes in the white thick clouds that had begun to rise trembling over the mountains to the east. The cigarette was bitter and stale from being carried around or cached in his locker too long. He dropped it among the small stones at the bottom of the wall and thought about it until the blue smoke ceased rising. He picked up the dirty white tennis shoes and the towel-wrapped clothes and the books. With the other hand he shoved himself off the wall and stood looking across town toward where the aspens lined the streets, gray-green and still. "Goddam son of a bitch."

Jolly ran his hand along the impersonal dark gray stones of the church as he rounded the corner and approached the front door. Once there, he took his penknife from his pocket, and balancing the tennis shoes atop his books, he opened the short blade. With his shoulder against one of the double doors he inserted the knife blade between them and pushed in on a small metal peg until it sprang back and its mate popped forward. He folded in the knife blade against his leg and replaced it in his pocket. Taking hold of the door handle he pulled once, hard, and the two doors swung open with a loud crack as the inside chain catch was forced from its niche. He closed but did not lock the doors from the inside and climbed the stairs to the sanctuary. The sun filtered through the yellow-glassed windows and created a false sunshine over the pulpit and pews, homely and quiet.

He walked resolutely to the front of the church. He set his school items on the front pew. He lifted the lid of the piano bench and took out his three books of piano music, which he stacked on the music holder of the black, square grand piano that squatted there in its ebony glory, a gift from someone long forgotten, someone, like the piano, from the nineteenth century.

Its rheumatic legs bowed down into lion's claws, each of which held a glass ball as tenaciously as if they were jungle delicacies newly captured.

Usually when he played the church piano he played quietly so that no passing pillar would hear him and enter to investigate. This day it did not matter. He started at the beginning of his books of Chopin nocturnes and played them in succession with little attempt at accuracy. They were too difficult for him at best, and he played too loudly and, he knew, badly. His left hand was cramped from carrying the school books, and the accompaniments that Chopin had doubtless intended to be winsome only thumped, disjointed and irregular, against the right hand melodies.

He had played for perhaps a half hour, taking greater pleasure from crashing the chords as they came, seeing nothing either in his mind or out of it—except the heavily blacked filigree of the pages—when he felt the hand placed lightly on his shoulder. Even before his eyes focused on the hand directly—a strong hand with long blunt fingers, pale-skinned against which the hair lay thick and black—he knew whose it was.

Jolly lifted his foot from the pedal and the discordant notes died, except for their faint echo on the stone walls of the church. "Hello, Jamie."

The hand tightened on his shoulder, then relaxed. "Sounds like Chopin and that man-woman—what's her name—had another fight."

Jolly turned sideways on the bench. "George

Sand,'' he said. ''I know. I never could play his stuff. Or anything else for that matter.''

''What are you doing here beating that piano to death?''

''I just don't feel so hot, I guess.'' Jolly struck a chord with his left hand. ''How'd you find me here?''

''I saw you come in and followed you.'' That was not the exact truth, but it was truthful enough. Actually, he had been sitting astride the chair facing the back, his chin on his folded arms, staring out the window into the bright bleakness of the street when he saw Jolly pass beside the church and around the corner to the front. A few minutes later he had heard faintly the sound of the piano. He was alone in the apartment, except for the child, who slept deeply and sprawled in his crib, because Mandy had already gone to work. What his thoughts were when Jolly intercepted his line of vision probably not even he knew. Possibly he wondered why he stayed here in this loud and dottering town with its four-square streets bordered by mongrel façades of glass brick and neon and yellow tile standing in haphazard discipline before the buildings that had once shaded the red carriage of the Territorial Governor on his way from his afternoon game at The Tree Frog to his split-log mansion.

''Oh,'' said Jolly. He faced the piano again. His fingers dawdled.

Jamie paced the width of the church and back to the center. His glance scanned the single circular window above the baptistry whose magenta and blue and gold glass cast foreshortened fragments of color across the carpeted floor and purled the edge of the single step down from the pulpit.

"This where you and Mom go?" he asked.

"Yes."

Jamie sat on the first bench behind Jolly, his hands jammed into his front pockets, his legs stretched out, crossed at the ankles.

"What do you come here for? I mean, now—like this."

"No reason. The piano, I guess."

He watched the back of Jolly's head for a moment, then let his own back against the edge of the bench. He stared at the high raftered ceiling from which hung the church lights on long brass chains.

"What's eatin' you, anyway."

"Nothing."

"You sure are friendly. What happened to all the talk?"

Jolly flipped a page of the book. He leaned his left elbow on the top edge of the piano and began to pick out the melody. He did not answer.

"Well, Jesus Christ!" Jamie flung himself up from the bench. He sat down again, abruptly. He propped his chin in his hands and eyed the round window as if it might explode daggers of glass for his insurrection.

"You moping about the same girl? Or another one," he said.

Jolly laughed, once, in spite of himself. "Another one, I guess."

Jamie waited. "Well? Go ahead."

"No." Jolly turned. "Only—one thing—you're right."

"What does that mean?" Jamie shifted his position on the bench. "I don't suppose I can smoke in here, can I?"

"No."

"No. Well, what do you mean?"

"You were right. Take any one of them whenever you can and get it before somebody else does."

"You still talking about girls?"

"Yes."

"I never said anything like that." Jamie's voice lost its flippant hem. Then he smiled. "You're out of your mind. I always thought so."

Jolly babbled the topmost keys of the piano. "Maybe," he said.

"Joll, you know I'm kidding."

"I know."

"You're wrong. I didn't say anything like that."

"No, you didn't say it. But you—you lived it. You know damn well you did. You always have. Traipsing all over the damn country years on end. And I know. Getting it wherever you could from anybody you could, and did you ever think that—"

"Knock it off, Jolly."

"—that maybe I—maybe somebody around here might want— Forget it. You're right. I said you were right."

Jamie was standing beside him. "Listen, you moron, you don't know what you're talking about." He clenched Jolly's shoulder with one hand. "Do you hear? You don't know what you're talking about!"

"Ouch!"

Jamie jerked back his hand and jammed it into his pocket again. He paced across the front of the room to where the stained glass laced a gilt edge on the floor.

"Well, don't preach at me. If you can do that—if you can sleep with them all and get up and hitch up your pants and walk out, well so can I. And I will. Goddamit, I will—"

"Shut up!" Jamie's shout reverberated against the gray stone. He came closer to Jolly. "I'm not preaching. God knows I'm not the one." His hands went to either side of Jolly's face and then his shoulders. "Listen, you know where I've been since the last time? Do you know where I've been? I'm going to tell you, and it's not going to do you any good, but it's going to maybe do me some good, and you're going to listen and then you're not going to say anything about it. Not to me or anybody.

"When I left here I knocked around some. Taking whatever windfalls there were. I landed in Gallup, and that's a dirty, stinking mud-hole, and then I took a job on a ranch about thirty or forty miles south of there. It was a pretty good ranch. Or could have been. The land was OK, just that everybody on the whole goddamned place was either no good or crazy. Or both. Even old Tampkens who owned the place. He was the worst. He is—or was—a near giant in his day, I guess, only now he walks hunched on two canes and drags his feet and you couldn't see anything of his face much.

Only eyes stuck in all that filthy hair. But he could get around. He couldn't ride a horse, or anything like that, but he could get around. And he could use those canes for something more than walking. He beat the horses with them, or the dogs, or whatever got in his way. Including his old woman, I guess. Anyway, at night sometimes we'd hear her and him up at the big house carrying on. He'd be yelling and she'd be screaming. We none of us ever knew what was going on, but the old woman never did anything in the daytime but sit out in back under a chinaberry tree and fan herself and shake her head and talk. Not to anybody. Just talking.

"It was a pretty good job. Not too much to do because, like I said, nobody worked very hard at ranching, and there were lots of hands. The pay was all right and there wasn't anything to spend it on except tail. Yeh, there's the funny part. The real funny part. There were these two Mexican girls that cooked and cleaned and stuff, and the old man's daughter—poor crazy thing like her mother, only an Amazon and ugly as hell—and his boy. We could have anything on the place, including the boy, I guess, if we'd wanted him. Except the old bastard's Indian girl that he kept up at the house.

"Anyway, Tampkens would sit out on his back porch every night and wait, rocking in that infernal homemade chair of his that you could hear squeaking the whole time you were in there. He'd sit there and wait for the men to come up from the bunkhouse to the girls' rooms there at the back of the house. And then on payday he'd keep out two bucks for every trip you made. Unless you picked the Amazon. Then it wasn't but a dollar. But nobody picked her much, which made the old man sore, but she was crazy, like I said, and the men didn't hanker much to her anyway, unless they knew next payday was already short, because she'd near killed a little guy a year before when she was first starting and lost her head and almost crushed him to death with her legs.

"I asked the other men some about the Indian girl. They didn't know anything about her. Just keep away, they said, if I knew what was good for me. And so I kept away. Until I couldn't any more.

"I'd been there four or five months before I ever really saw her up close. I was just passing one evening about sundown, back from the outhouse, and there she was throwing out feed in the chicken yard. She had the feed held up in one of those long, shiny skirts she wore, and was sort of talking, low like, to the chickens. I just stopped there by the fence and watched her. You see, the sun, slanting the way it was, made her skin like —like copper, maybe, or rose-gold like these windows, and her hair soft so you wanted to touch it. I just stood there, leaning on that chicken-wire fence till she came around by me. And then she looked up and kind of hollered. But quiet. Then she smiled. And Joll, her teeth and her eyes. You've never seen—you'll never see anything like that. I hadn't meant for anything to happen. I hadn't, but it sure-God did anyway. Even after dark when she knew the old son-of-a-bitch would be looking for her, we stayed down there in the grass by the creek. A long time.''

Jamie's voice stopped for a moment. The variegated stains spilled magenta and blue and gold slowly across the floor.

''We went on that way for two or three weeks, I guess, meeting down there in the long grass after she fed the chickens. Sometimes we didn't do anything. Sometimes we just sat there and watched the sky turn colors and pale-out until dark came. We would talk, too. Or more, she listened and I talked. You know something funny? Even when I left there, even when— I still don't know anything about her. Nothing but her name. Not where she came from, or how she came to be there. Nothing beyond those times by the creek, and then later, when we lived together.

''We lived together, the Indian girl and me, for five months. Five months. The old man let us fix up one of the sheds and live on there at the place. I should've known then when he let us fix up the shed and move in. I should've known something when I told him in the first place. He'd just laughed. Laughed like an idiot. The only time he ever laughed out loud that I know of except—except there at the end. He'd laughed and said she was going to have a baby—his—that she was three or four months already. I didn't know that, but I said I knew that and it didn't matter.'' Jamie chuckled, once, to himself. ''I must have looked like a goddamned peacock standing there on the back porch facing that old rotten bastard in his old rotten chair, saying how I knew and I didn't care and how I wanted her anyway.

And I did. God, I did. She was like nothing you'll ever see. She was tall and light on her feet and that same copper brown all over and quiet and better to me than anybody ever was to her.

"Whenever I saw Tampkens after that, which wasn't any oftener than I could help, he'd just laugh, only not out loud. You couldn't hear anything, but you could see his eyes wrinkle up and his shoulders would shake. I hated him then. I hated him so much I could have killed him, but I'm glad I didn't. I'm glad, because he's worse off alive. And I hope he lives a hundred years until the flesh drops off his rotten bones while he can't do anything but sit there in his chair and watch it drop."

Jolly watched him pace back into the light that emblazoned his legs with gorgeous colors.

"She swelled up big, of course. And I knew what I'd gotten, but I hated to see her swell up like that and it not mine. But I'd made my bargain, and I guessed I could stick to it. Only I didn't know and she didn't know. And the old man laughing to himself.

"Maybe if she'd been a white woman I'd have known she was sick as she was. She was always quiet anyway, and I never heard her complain about the housework, if you could call that a house, or the work she went on doing around the place, feeding the chickens and things, though she didn't have to. Her face was more beautiful, if that's possible, as her time came on.

"It wasn't until two or three weeks before the baby —before it came, that I found her one evening when I came in from work, lying on the bed and she couldn't get up. And she never did get up after that except when I helped her, when I nearly carried her a few steps around the shack every day. I should have gone into Gallup and got a doctor anyway. But she didn't want one. She said she'd be all right. She said she knew how to take care of things, and the Mexican girls came down every day and helped some and they said they knew all about babies being born, and that she'd be OK. Only they didn't know. But the old man knew.

"It was born one afternoon late, just after we'd come in from work and the men had gone to the well to wash up. When I walked in the shack I knew it was coming. She hadn't yelled out or anything—she didn't the whole time until the end—but her legs were twisting on the bed, and her lip was bleeding where she'd bitten it, and her face and hair were wet on the pillow. I don't remember what I did really, but the next thing, the Mexican girls were down there in the shack gibbering and crossing themselves and running back to the big house for water and rags and scissors and stuff. It was coming wrong, they said, and god, god, it must have hurt her. Sometimes she passed out and I wished she'd never come to so it wouldn't hurt her.

"Finally it began to come out, and I couldn't stand her eyes on me like that, and her sweating and bleeding at the mouth, and I reached in with my hands and pulled it out. Then she screamed once.

"It was in my hands.

"God, not in the worst nightmare did I ever know anything like that could come from a human being and that person still be alive. It was a baby, all right, I guess, but it was all blood and open sores and you couldn't see its face except a mouth, for the one pus-like mess that mashed its face all together into something like—like I don't know what. You couldn't tell was it a boy or girl because that part and all down its legs was eaten away too, and bloody, and you could see the bare white muscles in its legs move where the meat was gone, when it kicked.

"I laid it down on the bed there while I cut the cord. And then I slapped one of the Mexicans and left a bloody streak across her face to get her to stop praying long enough to work on the woman.

"I put it on the table and poured alcohol on a rag to hold over its face. It didn't take but a few seconds for it to stop kicking. It wouldn't have lived anyway, but it might have."

Jamie's voice dropped almost too low to hear. "And that would have been unspeakable beyond the telling of it.

"Then I took it in my hands out of the shack without looking back, and walked with it up to the big house just as the sky was coloring beyond the creek bank, up to the back porch where the old man sat rocking and watching me come. I put it down on his lap and I said, 'There's your baby,' and I walked away. I could hear him laughing and that goddamned chair squeaking even clear down at the corral.

"I rode away from there that night. I don't know much else that happened, other than the car, and California, and the doctors. They say I'll be OK," Jamie laughed. "They say I'll probably be just fine. Lucky, they say."

Jolly watched the pale hands approach his face.

"Don't jump," Jamie said. "They're clean. The doctors said they're clean." He drew Jolly up from the bench until their faces nearly touched. "Understand, Jolly. It wasn't what the old man had known and done anyway that matters. It wasn't what I had to do to—to the baby that matters. But I didn't even go back in there. She loved me, I know it, and I didn't even go back. I could have done that. She must have waked up sometime and wondered why I wasn't there. I could have done that much, for the two hours or the two days or the two weeks she would have lived. That's what matters. I loved her and she was dying and I ran."

Jamie's fingers relaxed. He fumbled in his shirt pocket for a cigarette and then put it back.

"I guess there's nothing—no moral or anything like that—in this, and I told you there wasn't. But when you start talking about what I've been up to, and the other night, when you were talking about that girl and about visiting the old place—well, I needed to tell, Joll. I've been back to the old place, too. I've seen it like it is now, only mostly I've seen it like it was. I've seen it days and nights all over this country.

"That used to be the past, the good past, and it was there to remember whenever you needed it. That and the good things you did—or you thought they were good—with the guys you ran with and the girls. Only, when something big happens, something big and maybe awful like what happened over there, then that's the past. The good past is like it's been wiped away like you clean off a blackboard, and you take your chances, will the new be beautiful like the old, or rotten. You've got to do it. Nobody can stop it. But you take your chances."

Jamie's voice stopped. He stepped up beside the oak pulpit, faced the round window and laughed. His white shirt and black pants were splashed with harlequin triangles of magenta and blue and gold.

FOURTEEN

"THERE'S the goddam border, men," said Guppy. "It won't be long now."

"Where?" asked Jolly, sitting up straighter in the back seat.

"There," said Al Burgess beside him. "See those gates?"

"Yeh. Is that the border?" Somehow he believed crossing the border into a foreign country should be more momentous. Here there were simply two lanes for traffic going each way under an overhanging roof, much like driving into a gas station. Running in either direction from the inspection stations was a high wire fence topped with three strands of barbed wire, tilted toward the Mexican side.

A perspiring Mexican official waved them through without question, his face impassive behind a full black moustache. Crossed over his brown uniform shirt were two leather belts, and around his waist a gun belt with pistol. "You're in Mexico now, Fingers. Gettin' back across is harder than gettin' in," Guppy laughed maliciously. "But you'll be glad you decided to join this little band."

The highway turned and narrowed into a main street of the town. Although it was nearly midnight there were a number of people on the brightly neoned street. Little knots of men squatted or stood about on the sidewalks, their shapes and faces indistinguishable from one another, against a background of yellow-stuccoed saloons from which loud Mexican versions of American music shrieked through open doors, meeting and mixing with like sounds from across the street.

Near the corner, beside the wide hotel doors of the Fray Marcos de Niza, sat a little boy on his shoeshine box, his head asleep on his folded arms, his bare feet tucked as far back as possible in the hope they wouldn't be trampled on. If he stayed late enough perhaps one more *Americano* passing in or out of the tall hotel would shake him and ask for a shine.

Along the next street most of the shops and markets were closed for the night, but a few remained dimly lighted. Their proprietors leaned in the doorways in white shirts and talked with one another. The next day they would all be open early in anticipation of the tourists who might be cajoled into buying a cheap silver trinket, or a facsimile *bandillero,* or a hand-tooled leather purse.

"We gotta remember to buy some booze before we go back," said Guppy. "You ever had any a this Mexican hootch, Fingers?"

"Yeh, sure," he lied. "It's pretty good."

"Goddam right. And you can buy a gallon a the horse piss for less'n five bucks. Jesus Christ!" Guppy swerved to miss a taxicab that convulsed down the street astraddle the center line, its horn blaring continuously. "These goddam spics drive like cars ain't been invented yet."

Jolly watched the neon lights grow fewer as Guppy negotiated the midnight traffic past the central part of the town. The big saloons and shops gave way to tiny adobe buildings that could have been one-room houses. In some of them lights shone through curtainless windows upon customers seated at a table or a small counter, drinking tequila or eating tamales and beans.

Guppy turned onto a dark dirt road that from all appearances would lead nowhere. "We're almost there," Al Burgess said to Jolly, his words low on his breath. Jolly's stomach tightened the same way it had for the last two days whenever he thought of this trip with Guppy and Al and Eddie Culp. He had spent some time imagining what it would be like—Canal Street, the nightclubs and all—but no clear picture came, and it would be embarrassing to ask anyone.

The road dipped and turned back on itself, and there in a brilliance of neon stretched Canal Street, unpaved, but wider and more blazing than any street in town. "There she is!" howled Guppy to the night.

"Jeez, it's beautiful," said Jolly, surprised. The remark brought hoots of laughter from the others. "Yeh, and it's beautiful what they do to you in bed, too!"

Guppy drove midway down the block and parked among several dozen cars that lined the street before places named The Cabana Club, or El Toro, or The Mickey Mouse Cantina. Leaning in the doorways of many, or seated on the low window sills, were

Mexican women who called short shrill greetings to the cars that passed slowly along the street. In the semi-dark little could be seen of them but the outlines of their long, fluffed hair and their bodies tightly curved into satin dresses or ruffled in native blouses and full spangled skirts. Their voices sounded happy and set for fun. A strolling band of *mariachis* interwove their hybrid voices and guitars from the sidewalk with the gay amplified music of the bands and jukeboxes inside the clubs. The green and blue and red neon winked and chattered welcome.

"Come in, boys," one of three women called from the doorway of La Cantina. Her voice was not harsh, but too familiar.

"OK, baby," said Guppy. As he passed first through the door he lay the flat of his hand across the woman's chest, bare in a wide expanse of skin that glowed yellowly in the light. She flicked away his hand as lightly as she would a fly and said something in Spanish to her companions. The three giggled.

Inside, La Cantina was comprised of one large square room along one side of which ran a bar with white-coated bartenders moving phlegmatically behind it, their black hair in long polished curls above their young faces. Jutting out to nearly the center of the room was a raised dance floor. The band, enshrouded within a sort of three-sided cabana, played every note at fullest volume, two brassy trumpets duplicating a Latin melody above a bevy of guitars and rattled, shook, scraped, or crashed rhythm instruments. Bright yellow lights shone on the deserted dance platform and faded into blue eclipse along the far side of the room and in the corners.

"Now, Fingers," Guppy said, launching one great arm over Jolly's shoulders, "don't buy a drink for ever' bitch that asks ya, and don't go off in the tules with the first one. Remember, the best ones are busiest, and ya might hafta look around good first." Guppy's speech didn't mean much to Jolly. It really made little sense at all to him, but he found a place and stored the advice along with a good deal of other new knowledge that had hit him in the last five minutes.

Most of the small tables crowded about the room were occupied. At several sat couples, usually two couples, their heads together, laughing. At one table they edged past, Jolly saw a black-haired girl sitting on a young sailor's lap, her head tilted behind his, her eyes closed. He was startled to see the sailor's face laid against her chest, his eyes gazing blindly at one bare breast he held up from her blouse, cupped in his hand.

"Jeez, did you see *that!*" he whispered to Eddie Culp.

"That ain't nothin'," said Eddie. "You ain't seen nothin' yet."

Sitting at some of the tables were lone girls and women, never more than two at a table, languidly smoking cigarettes or sipping small green drinks, their eyes moving steadily over the men and boys as they entered the room. Occasionally one or both would rise and move to a table at which sat two or three customers.

Sometimes they sat with the customers; sometimes they moved back to their own tables.

"Here," said Guppy. "Let's set here." He pulled back a chair from an empty table close to the edge of the dance platform. "They oughta be havin' a show perty soon." No one objected to Guppy's choice of table, nor to the order he gave the waiter. *"Cerveza,"* he said. "Carta Blanca."

"Four?" the waiter asked.

"Yeh. *Quatro cervezas,"* said Guppy.

"Don't they care how old you are here?" asked Jolly.

"Hell, no," said Eddie Culp smiling. "You can have anything in the house if you got the money." He winked at Jolly.

The band stopped playing and a short hefty man in a pale blue flannel suit with wide lapels and full, almost bloused trousers walked quickly to the center of the dance platform carrying a small microphone in one hand, and with the other he held the black cord to the side so he wouldn't step on it. He addressed the crowd first in Spanish and then in English.

"Hot damn. The floor show's gonna start," said Guppy.

Their waiter arrived with four beers in short, pale bottles. "One dollar," he said.

The band began again, louder than ever, a fast tune accentuated with much hammering and scraping of native instruments. From through the curtains beside the band there entered a tall, smiling woman, her head thrown back proudly, entirely encased from neck to toes in a tight black velvet gown that just matched her hair and that she wore as she stepped around the perimeter of the platform once.

"God, she's beautiful," said Jolly.

"You ain't seen nothin' yet," said Eddie, his eyes on the woman in black.

As if by magic the black gown fell completely away from the woman's body, and she kicked it back toward the band. The room filled with shrill whistles and shouts.

"Christ, they get down to brass tacks in a hurry here, don't they!" shouted Guppy. "Off with the rest, baby!" His voice rose over the general din.

Jolly watched incredulously as the music shifted to a slow, heavily accented beat, and the woman paced about the platform, skipping slightly on every first beat, her body and arms swaying with exaggeration. When she turned again she held in one hand the red fringe that had encircled her hips, but to the disappointment of her audience, the red fringe had concealed but another, narrower one.

Jolly was unaware of the voice at his ear until she placed a hand on his arm and spoke more loudly. He turned to find his face not four inches from that of a woman leaning down beside him and was aware all together of her beaded eyelashes, the dark powder over wrinkles, and a heavy scent of perfume and perspiration. Her hair hung long on her shoulders, curled in a style long out of fashion (at least in Cortez), dyed dark red except near her skull where it was black.

"What?" said Jolly, drawing back his face. "What did you say?"

"You got cigarette for me?" She minced her words.

Jolly looked toward Guppy and Al and Eddie, but their backs were to him, their attention on the dancer who continued to peel off bits of fringe and glitter. He turned back to the woman. "Sure. Sure, I got a cigarette." He pulled one from his pack. "You need a light?"

She only smiled and held the cigarette to her lips. She sat, slowly, on the edge of the vacant chair between Jolly and Guppy. She leaned forward to meet the match Jolly extended after some fumbling, and his eyes followed the cleavage of her breasts until it disappeared at what he believed was the last possible instant.

Guppy chose that moment to whirl around and shout "God! Look at them—" He stopped when he saw the woman beside Jolly. His mouth closed slowly over an unformed word. "Jesus Christ, Osment. I *told* you not to let the first one get to you. What the hell'r you doing?"

"Nothing," Jolly said. "I—that is, she just asked for a cigarette."

"Oh, my God." He looked the woman over. She continued to watch Jolly's face. "Scram, you old bitch," Guppy said. "Beat it. Get your worn-out ass outa here."

"Guppy, you can't—you shouldn't talk like that to a *wo*man, for God's sake," said Jolly.

"Shit," Guppy snorted. "You!" He punched her on the upper arm. "Beat it! Vamoose!" He waved his hand in her face.

She turned to Guppy and spoke rapidly in Spanish, her words clipped and angry.

"What did she say?"

"Hell, how should I know? Get rid of her, Fingers. She's old enough to be my grandmother. Git!" he spat, as one would talk to a chicken.

She watched Jolly closely and smiled. She leaned close to his ear and said "Forky me?"

"What?"

She laughed. "Forky me. Three dollars?"

The meaning of the request outlined Jolly's mind once and then came to roost squarely. He looked to Guppy. "My God. Did you hear—" but Guppy's attention was on the lady of the very little clothes. Jolly drank from the beer bottle slowly. The beer was warm and tasted flat. He looked at the table and shook his head. "No," he said. "No."

From the corner of his eye he saw her hand grind the cigarette in the ashtray, and then he felt her rise from the chair and withdraw, leaving only the heavy sweet perfume. Jolly let out his breath and raised his eyes to the platform where the dancer was making her final pop-out from between the curtains, totally nude. She wiggled her brown behind to the audience and disappeared. The applause was clamorous and blatant, but short-lived.

Al Burgess was silent, as usual, but Guppy and Eddie swung back around in their chairs and exchanged comments on the varied abilities and endowments of the dancer. The lights grew gradually brighter, and the band members dispersed through the curtains.

"Let's get outa here," said Guppy. He tilted back his head and drank from the beer bottle until it was empty. He set it on the table and shoved back his chair. "Let's go looking," he said.

Out on the board sidewalks again, Jolly breathed gladly of the night air. "God, that's a noisy place," he said.

Guppy laughed. "Al, you and Eddie didn't see, but old Fingers came damn close to fallin' in back there. Jolly," he added earnestly, "we ain't here to make international *friends,* fer chrissake. Don't pay no attention to them old bags. They's plenty a good, young ones, but like I say, they're workin' hardest an' ya gotta look for 'em." He marched at the head of his little troop, surveying the likelihood of each club entrance as they passed. The door-standers spoke to them, sometimes gaily, sometimes sullenly. Jolly walked on the outside, away from the buildings. "Here's the place," Guppy said finally. "You remember, Al? We had a helluva time here last trip."

"Yeh," said Al.

"What was that one's name? You know—Maria, or something?"

"Melinda," said Al.

Guppy entered the club. "Yeh," he said. "I sure hope she's still here."

This club was smaller and lighter. There was no dance platform and no band. Across the room, near two tables where five boys wearing university sweaters were drinking beer and laughing quietly with five of the black-haired girls, a *mariachi* trio played quiet guitar music. The room was decorated with Mexican tin wall ornaments, ritual masks mostly, and with several painted murals done in flat bright colors with the figures of gauchos and beflowered señoritas in the typical Mexican distortion. It was not crowded, yet there were six or eight unoccupied girls sitting at the tables, besides the couples and quartets at other tables or on the high stools at the bar.

"*Quatro cervezas,*" said Guppy, straddling a chair turned backward to the table. "Carta Blanca."

As the beer was served they were joined by two girls from a nearby table, and then a third. They were all younger than those in the previous place, and one of the three was actually pretty but wore heavy purple lipstick.

"This is more like it," said Eddie, moving his legs from under the table and patting them to indicate to the girl at his side that she was to sit there.

"Set down, baby," said Guppy, drawing a chair near to him. The girl smiled and asked for a drink. "Sure, baby," he said and cupped his hand under her near breast. She giggled and removed his hand, drawing it beneath the table to her thigh.

Al did not offer the third girl a chair. Instead, without speaking, he stood, and taking the girl by the hand he led her across the room to a blue door through which they disappeared.

Guppy laughed. "Well, I guess Al's the first one down tonight." His other arm encircled the girl's neck, and his hand came to rest on her other breast, where it stayed.

Jolly drank his beer, which was colder than the first but still distasteful to him. Eddie and Guppy had their minds fully occupied. He heard the girl on Eddie's lap laugh at something he had whispered to her. He watched as she slipped her hand down beside her own hip, between Eddie's legs. "You big," she said and laughed again.

Supposing that that activity was something one did not watch openly, even in a Mexican whorehouse, Jolly turned away and scanned the room. His eyes alighted on a girl seated a little distance away, by herself. She was staring directly at him, and her eyes did not waver as he looked at her. Jolly smiled for no reason other than habit. The girl did not smile, but she pulled another chair back from the table a few inches and stared.

He walked to the girl's table and said, *"Buenas noches,"* and then felt ridiculous. "Hi," he said.

She smiled then. "Hello," she said. "Sit down?"

"OK." He sat on the chair stiffly. "Would you like a cigarette or anything? A drink?"

Her laugh trembled darkly for a moment. "No, *gracias,"* she said, and Jolly had the feeling she spoke English as well as she did Spanish. "What is your name?"

"Jolly."

"Jolly?" she repeated. The "j" was softer than he had said it.

He laughed. "That's close. What's your name?"

"Oh," she said and wiped a spot of wet from the table with her finger, "I am called Dolores."

"That's a pretty name. I like that." The conversation lagged. Jolly drank from his beer and started all over again. "Sure you wouldn't like something?"

"*Qué?*" She lifted her eyebrows. "What?"

"Never mind." He traced a circle and two dots on the wet side of his bottle. She folded her hands on the table and spoke. "You have come before, here, yes?"

"Huh? Oh, no." He watched the slender fingers clasp and unclasp. "No, I haven't—I have not." He followed the brown skin up her arm to her bare shoulder.

"Do you live here? In Nogales, I mean," he said.

She tilted her head and viewed him quizzically.

"Is this town your home?" he said.

"No." Her eyes returned to her hands. "My home is Guadalajara, except this half year."

"I know that song," Jolly said. " 'Guadalajara, Guadalajara, la la la la la,' " he sang, "or something like that." She laughed, and it rose from deep in her throat and spilled upwards. She wore a pale green dress of some light material that crossed behind her neck leaving her back bare to the waist.

Jolly moved his chair closer. He touched her shoulder because the brown skin there needed touching. "How old are you, Dolores?" he asked and traced the curve of her shoulder with one finger. Her skin twitched involuntarily beneath his finger so he stopped. He placed the flat of his hand on her back. "How many years are you?"

Her hair was dark brown, not black like the others. It was pulled back from her face and clasped simply in back. "I have eighteen years." She raised her chin, and her eyes bespoke brief defiance.

Jolly lifted her hair from off her neck and watched it stream over his hand. "So am I—nearly," he said. With his other hand he touched hers on the table. "You have pretty hands."

She looked at the backs of her hands as if she were about to argue the point. Instead she smiled a very small bit at the corners of her mouth. "Thank you," she said.

His knee touched hers. He expected hers to draw back quickly, but instead he felt her leg press closer to his. She leaned nearer over the corner of the table, and the light material swung forward an inch from her breasts. Jolly could see that it was unlikely she wore anything beneath the dress. Her brown skin rose glowing and round.

He raised his eyes and met hers. To hide his blush he pulled her towards him, and with his lips at her neck just below her ear he closed his eyes and said, "You're lovely."

He felt her move against him. Then he felt her remove her hand from his on the table. As the hand slid heavily up the inside of his thigh to where he was urgent, she said clearly, "Forky me, three dollar."

The warmth went out of the moment as suddenly as if winter had struck in May. Jolly heard the sounds of the club return, and when he opened his eyes, over her shoulder he saw bare wooden tables and beer bottles and young men mauling black-haired girls in two's and three's.

They moved their heads back at the same time so that when their eyes met, their faces were close. Jolly studied her eyes but saw nothing except a chill that matched the room. She did not speak again but waited for his response. Her eyes were lighter brown, like her hair. And then Jolly saw the gold flecks in her eyes that caught the light and radiated from the black iris.

He moved back in his chair and expelled his breath. "OK," he said. "Let's go."

She stood and without looking back strode across the room, her head high, toward the blue door. Jolly heard Guppy call something to him, but he did not answer. He walked behind Dolores and wondered, incongruously, that her waist was thicker than it should have been.

Before they could pass through the blue door at the corner of the room, they had to squeeze by two round girls in peasant blouses and full black skirts who stood in the open door of the men's room giggling and chattering with two university boys who were attempting to drown a black beetle with urine in the trough that ran along the floor. Once through the blue door, they walked down a long corridor, open to the sky above, but lined on either side with rooms, each with its own door and a single window. From some of the windows no light shone, and from some came the short sounds of laughter.

Near the end of the corridor, Dolores unlocked a door and entered ahead of Jolly. He heard her fumble in the dark a moment, then a match flared, and she lighted four candles in an elaborate tin candelabrum. He stood just inside the door and saw the small room pale into half-light. The window was covered with orange-flowered chintz as was the opening to what must have been a closet. In one corner there was a sink, and beneath it stood a white pitcher in a porcelain bowl. In another corner, on a spindly three-legged table, stood an icon, its garish colors faintly illuminated by a single candle burning low in a red glass holder. He looked away from the corner quickly, but not before the candle, fed by new air in the room, sputtered upward and lighted the word *Inri* near the top of the small gold cross.

"Take off your clothes." Dolores spoke deliberately as she unfastened the side of her dress.

The only other pieces of furniture in the room were a blond wooden dresser on which stood the candelabrum, one straight chair, and a double bed made up with no covers other than a bare sheet and two pillows.

Jolly turned from the girl and undressed hurriedly, down to his shorts. He wondered if it would be all right to leave his socks on. He pondered that problem as he hung his shirt and pants over the chair, being careful that the things did not spill from the pockets. Behind him he heard the girl moving swiftly. "Light?" she said.

"What?"

"Do you wish light? The candles I can leave on or off?" she said.

"Oh. OK, they're OK."

"Come," she said.

He turned to see her lie on the bed and adjust a pillow beneath her head, her legs spread brownly on the white sheets. His eyes followed the curves of her body. And then he saw.

"Won't it—won't this harm it?"

"What?" she asked. Her voice was sharp.

"I said, is it all right—to do this when you're—when you're that way?" He pointed vaguely with his hand.

She twisted impatiently beneath his gaze.

"*Hurry,*" she said, and her voice had turned cold like the night.

FIFTEEN

THE STATUE of Teddy Roosevelt and his pawing steed exactly matched the gray-green of the aspens when the four boys returned to Cortez as the sun was making its first pale overtures against the clouds in the east. The trip home had been fast and silent except for Guppy's occasional comments on the conditions in Nogales. Jolly watched sleepily as the car passed the first familiar houses and motels that signaled the edge of town. The old courthouse seemed snug and comfortable squatted among its aspens in the plaza. The stores, which would not open for four hours yet, looked fresher, somehow, possibly because of the early light.

"Where to first?" said Guppy.

"Let's get some breakfast somewhere," said Eddie. "God, my mouth feels like the floor of a stable."

"It's too early to go home, anyway."

"Remember, Al, we stayed with you last night—and played poker."

"Yeh, I'll remember. Christ, I hope I get some sleep today before my folks get back."

"You gotta work today, Jolly?"

Jolly yawned. "Nope. All I want is some breakfast and a shower and a bed."

"A shower won't help what you got now," offered Guppy. "Penicillin's what you need."

A while later, after breakfast at Freddy's, Guppy drove the others to their homes. He stopped last before Jolly's house. Jolly viewed the rocky walk that led between the two pines. "I see the lilacs are starting," he said.

"What?" said Guppy.

"Nothing." He turned to the big shaggy-haired boy beside him. "Thanks, Guppy—for letting me go along."

"That's OK." Guppy rolled down the window on his side. "Jolly—was it—did ya like it and all?"

"Yeh, sure. Sure I liked it OK. Why?"

Guppy flushed. He put one huge hand on Jolly's shoulder. "Oh, nothin'," he said. "It's just that you're a couple a years younger than us guys and all. You were sorta quiet and everything." He watched Jolly's face for a moment. "Maybe I shouldn't a—maybe you—Oh, hell, ferget it," he concluded and returned his hand to the wheel. He revved the motor.

"So long, Hero," Jolly said. He left the car and heard it squeal and then roar away behind him as he climbed the path to his house.

"Well, you're up bright and early," his mother said when he opened the kitchen door. "You boys have a nice time?"

"Hi. Yeh, we had a swell time." He was relieved by the sound of her voice.

"What'd you-all do? Just play cards? I hope you weren't really gambling."

"Just matches, Mom." He walked to the bathroom door. "Jeez, I need a bath."

"You had breakfast?"

"Yeh. We went out to Freddy's. And, Mother, I had a *good* breakfast." He grinned and then closed the door.

She waited until she heard the water stop running. As she worked about the kitchen she talked, generally, to the bathroom door. "Listen, Jolly-Bo. I'm going to walk downtown before the heat and do a little shopping, you hear?"

"OK."

"And then I'm going on to my missionary circle. I may not be back before lunch, but they's cold ham and Jello in the icebox. You eat lunch before you go galavantin' off somewhere. Hear?"

He splashed from the bathroom.

Mattawilde Osment went to the bedroom to gather her hat and purse. She lifted the curtain at the window in order to calculate the mood of the weather. "Reckon I'd better take it," she said to herself and reached her old red umbrella from the closet. Back in the kitchen she said "I'm going now, Jolly-Bo. Now listen, if it rains, you go around and see the windows are closed." She waited a moment for an answer from the bathroom. "You asleep in there?"

"No. I heard you."

"Well, don't go to sleep in there, though Lord knows you look like you could stand some. Go to bed if you want to."

"OK. Goodbye, Mom."

Jolly lay in the hot bath water a long time, going over every portion of the night before, only now, in the light of a new day, the events, the talk, the black-haired girls and the brown-haired one all rolled together with the brassy music, the guitars, the ribald lights, the Carta Blanca and the chintz-curtained room at the end of a corridor beyond a blue door. He was surprised to realize that all he remembered about the first woman he had ever seen totally naked (besides the dancer) was her brown belly rising round, starting high at her waist. He closed his eyes better to focus the picture, and all he saw was her navel protruding, tight. Without reason his mind switched to the picture of a trocar, delving deep into the brown flesh, making another navel, one to which would be attached a plastic button. That would be a good new game; Button, button, who's got the new Bellybutton. Jolly felt the muscles in his stomach jerk. He opened his eyes with a start and stared for a long time up at the yellow ceiling, pulling back the pieces into reality.

He sat forward and pulled the chain and watched as the soapy water formed a tiny whirlpool over the drain. He stepped from the tub and dried himself, then separated his shirt and shorts and socks for the dirty clothes basket, and carrying his pants and shoes, he walked through the kitchen, through the dining room, into the bedroom.

Covered by only a sheet, he closed his eyes and slept a long, dreamless sleep.

In the early afternoon Jolly awoke to the sound of rain spattering in loud, seldom drops. "Mom, you here?" he called.

Hearing no answer, he stretched, then threw back the sheet, and with his feet on the floor, he sat a moment and rubbed his eyes, heavy with sleep. He checked the windows and stood by one to watch the dark spots of wet form gradually on the cement steps in front of the house. When the cement was thoroughly darkened, he turned from the window to the kitchen and rummaged in the refrigerator.

I'll just walk out there, he planned. It's not that far. I'll just walk out there and see. If it rains, well, it rains.

Fifteen minutes later, dressed in Levis and a Levi jacket, he crossed the alley and the oak-wooded lot behind his house and climbed the short hill to a road that would be the quickest way. The road was not yet particularly muddy. It would be in another hour, though, even with the slow rain. He figured to be there before an hour, anyway.

Once through the stone pillars, Jolly left the road and walked parallel to it, curving when it curved, hurrying across the narrow arteries that joined the main road, until he reached the one marked Paseo Redondo. From there he cut directly through the woods, his feet silent on the thickness of damp needles.

He wasn't sure what he would do when he got there. Likely, he would do nothing, he thought, except wait and watch. When the house came into sight, the color of the bark of the pines, he stopped. Then he circled until he had a fairly clear view of the front and the Van Dearens' green sedan. The house huddled in on itself, shedding rain in little streams from its peaked roof. Its face told nothing.

The Blue Goose wasn't there, at least. That was some comfort.

Jolly sat beneath a big pine that shielded him some from the rain. He lighted a cigarette and watched. He watched a long time, expecting to see he knew not what. Maybe she wasn't even there. Maybe she and Luke were away somewhere at that very moment. He drew himself tighter into his jacket and listened to the rain that sounded like faint laughter spilling.

The steady rain grew colder. But where would they go on an afternoon like this? Luke's mind functioned in terms of darkness. A rainy afternoon would mean nothing more to him than a rainy afternoon. Jolly grew a little stiff from sitting in one place so long and staring at the house. It took him several moments to realize that Mr. Van Dearen had just hurried from the house, his collar turned up, and into his car. Jolly sat forward to watch the green car back up and then point slowly down the driveway to the road. Through open spots in the woods he saw it move along the road, away from the house.

He stood and arched his back. He was more stiff than he should have been. He had sat longer than he thought. He moved among the trees, walking closer to the house. Finally, at the edge of the Van Dearens' lot from which the underbrush had been cleared, he made up his mind.

I can just say I was out for a walk and got caught in the rain, he decided.

He touched the side of the great granite boulder on which she sat and laughed—how long ago?—six days, it was. The board steps of the porch, saturated with rain, made no sound under his feet. He moved across the wide porch and knocked at the door.

Mrs. Van Dearen opened the door, and her eyes passed down from his hair, wet and bedraggled, over his rough clothes. "Yes?"

"Hello. Is—I was just walking by, and I got caught in the rain," he chanted. "That is, I *like* to walk in the rain and all, but—is Dogie here?" he finished.

The woman did not step back or ask him in. "She's sick."

"I know. I mean, that's part of the reason I stopped by. To see how she is."

"Are you Luke? Are you the one she was with last night?"

Jolly smiled. "No, ma'am. I'm Jolly. The watercress and stuff."

Mrs. Van Dearen relaxed her hold on the door somewhat. "She's sick," she said again. "But I guess you can talk for a minute."

"I'll just stay out here, if it's OK with you. My shoes are muddy and everything."

She considered for a moment. Then she said, "All right. She can come out—but only for a minute—if she wraps up." She closed the door.

Jolly leaned on the porch railing, his hands in his

pockets, and watched the closed door. In a few moments it opened again.

There she was.

There she was, her face peering out from under a red and black Navajo blanket that she held tightly to her, the end dragging behind. She lifted one arm, palm outward, and said "How!"

Jolly laughed. "Hello, crazy."

She let the blanket drop from around her head and shook the yellow hair so that it fell, rumpled, about her shoulders. "Hello, Jolly."

"Hi. How're you feeling? Your mom said you were real sick."

"Mother worries too much." She looked past him to the wet forest. "Isn't this beautiful?" she said.

"This rain?"

"Yes."

"Most people would say this is a pretty dull day."

"It's not. It's a wonderful day. I wish I could just walk and walk on a day like this, don't you?" She didn't know that walking in the rain was precisely what he had been doing. She came to stand beside him and leaned over the porch rail. Jolly saw the blue spot at her temple, like a patch of sky seen through thin clouds.

"I've *been* walking. How do you think I got here?"

She turned to him as if seeing him for the first time. "You are wet, aren't you. You'll catch cold and have to go around in an Indian blanket," she said, but she didn't smile. "What are you looking at?"

"Your eyes," he said. "The gold flecks—"

“The what?”

“The gold *flecks.* They’re gone.”

She faced the woods again. “Are they?” she said and fell silent.

“Dogie, I’d like to take you out again. I’d like to go somewhere with you.”

“No, Jolly.” She lifted her chin and drew in a deep breath. The bellows sound rasped. “Besides, I don’t think Mother will let me out for a while.”

“You were with Luke again last night, weren’t you.”

“Yes. Yes. Why do you look at me like that? I went out with Luke last night and the night before—and, who knows? I might again.” She smiled to herself.

“What’s Luke got—I mean, what’s so much better about Luke than me?”

“Nothing, Jolly. Nothing.”

“Then why?”

“Can’t we drop it?” she asked.

“No. I think I ought to know. I took you out first. I found you. You wanted to go to a wiener roast and I took you. And Dogie, I’d take you anywhere else you wanted to go.”

She drew the blanket tighter over her shoulders, her hands crossed over her chest. “I know, Jolly. And I appreciate it—”

“Appreciate it! Look, a guy doesn’t just—well, I mean, I’m not asking for appreci*a*tion, for God’s sake.” He turned away angrily. “I just don’t see why Luke’s so much better than I am.”

“It isn’t that, I’m trying to tell you,” she said, and her voice was nearly lost in the rain.

"Well, what, then? Just tell me." He faced her again and touched her shoulder. "Just tell me and I'll stop pestering you."

Her eyes lifted to meet his, and he noticed for the first time the dark smudges that hadn't been under her eyes four nights ago. "All right," she said. "I'll tell you. I'll tell you if you promise not—"

"Of course. What are you talking about?"

"Luke made love to me," she said.

"What do you mean, he made love to you?"

"I mean just that. The night before last. And last night."

Jolly stopped his tirade. He looked all over her face on which the freckles stood out against the flesh, over her hair the color of April laburnums, over her hands that held the blanket closely. He swallowed once and said, "Do you mean like—well, like Luke and Babe Wooten?" His mouth remained open, waiting.

She smiled, and some of the light returned to her eyes. "Yes, Jolly. Just like Babe Wooten."

"Son of a bitch," he said.

She watched him curiously. "How old are you, Jolly? Never mind, I know how old you are."

"I'm the same as him."

"No, you're not. Even if you are, you're not. And I'm eighteen. Does that surprise you?"

"Yes."

"It's because I'm little and have these idiot freckles." She breathed deeply again. "Eighteen years on that god-forsaken ranch with nothing but asthma and white-faced cows."

Jolly said nothing. His mind tumbled over firelight, and April laburnums and red fringes and a sunlit pond and a bare brown belly and a grinning boy with a shock of straight black hair.

"I'd better go in, Jolly," she was saying. "Jolly?"

"What?"

"I said I'm going in."

"OK." He walked to the top step of the porch. "OK, Dogie. So long."

He walked a long way through the pine woods, the rain soaking his clothes, until he reached the paved road. From the sanctuary of the trees he looked out upon the paved road that led, in one direction, toward town. The rain made the asphalt blacker and made it shine with polish. When a car traveled over the road its tires sucked away the polish and sent it spraying. As soon as the car was gone the rain began its patient re-surfacing of the tracks. Except for the occasional cars there was nothing to break the steady, shy sound of the rain that with each drop cleaned the pines and the years-deep rug of pine needles and the dwarf oaks. The air itself grew lighter, lifting the odors of the woods, sweeping the smell of burning fireplaces through the trees. In the ditches the Indian paintbrush raged red and defiant beside clumps of white daisies whose myriad heads salaamed in turn to the god rain.

Sheltered by the umbrella of a great pine, Jolly attempted to light a cigarette with matches grown soggy in his pocket. He deliberately struck each match on the little sandpaper strip until the pink heads had all been rubbed away. None of them would light. The cigarette had become wet, also, from being held between his lips too long, so he dropped it to the ground along with the matches. He leaned against the rough bark and waited. He was not waiting for the rain to stop. He was not waiting for darkness. If you had chanced upon him there, his hands shoved into his pants pockets and with his collar turned stiffly against the rain, and asked him why he waited, he would have been unable to tell you. As long as he stayed within the woods there were no complications. A man's (and likely a boy's) thoughts are his own in the forest. He can think whatever or wherever his mind will let him. And there is nothing to which he must give account for the things he thinks of or the things he does. Certainly the pines do not care. He may stand there, and welcome. But once he stands on a paved road he has to go somewhere, because a paved road was meant to go somewhere. If he chooses to walk the paved road he will come to people, eventually, because that is the somewhere a paved road goes.

He did not shiver until he saw the orange square of light appear across the road, deep among the trees. Some woman had begun to stir in her kitchen, preparing dinner. For a moment it seemed that the day was going backwards, or that a whole night had disappeared while he stood there, and this was a new morning in the making.

He slid down the short muddy bank part way, then leaped onto the pavement and stamped the mud from his shoes. He crossed to the left side of the road more for obscurity than for safety, and he hunched against the chill rain as he headed toward town.

He did not know what he would say to Luke. The realization that he wasn't angry had come a long time back, but he hadn't tried to reason that out. Maybe he wouldn't say anything at all about Dogie. She seemed to be far away, wrapped in the woods and her Indian blanket. Jolly stopped absent-mindedly in the rain. It was Luke's face, not Dogie's, that appeared in his mind. It was the dark-skinned face, not the freckled one, the slow grin, not the head thrown back in laughter, the straight black hair, not the yellow that appeared. It was Luke he wanted to see.

Jolly turned back on the road in the direction of home. His clothes were cold against his skin and wet. Gloaming came early on afternoons of rain when the setting sun, obscured, could not reflect its light from the eastern hills. His mother would have supper ready to serve already, he knew, because the evening meal was always served as night fell, not by the clock.

The car's lights picked and blinked over the wet trees and then the pavement before Jolly heard it. He stepped to the muddy bank and continued to walk without looking back. Just as the wet kiss of the tires was audible he recognized the valient, cardiographic pump of the Blue Goose's engine. He stopped and watched the car approach.

"Hey, Joll." The car door swung open.

"Hey, Luke." Jolly slid onto the seat.

"Where the hell you been? I been callin' you for about ten hours."

"You know where I've been."

"You seen Dogie?" Luke asked. He watched the road.

"Yeh, I saw her. You got any goddam dry matches?"

"No."

"Figures. What are you doing?"

"Turning around. We got a body to pick up."

"No," Jolly said. "I don't want to. I'm going home."

"Ah, jeez, Joll. It won't take long." Luke stopped the car cross-wise in the road and waited. "I'll need some help."

"Where is it?"

"County."

"There's lots of people to help out there." Jolly turned his face toward the right-hand window. "You gonna take me home? Because if you aren't, I'll get to walking again."

Luke grumbled and began to turn the car back the way it was first headed. "Yeh, I'll take you home. Jesus H."

They rode without talking for a while until Jolly faced Luke again and blurted, "Goddam you, Luke."

"Well, hell, Joll. You had your chance to—"

"You call that a chance?" Jolly's voice climbed high above the wet sounds of the car. "You call that a goddam *chance?* Right in the middle of a stinkin' cloudburst?"

Luke's voice was patient. "I told you, Joll, you gotta keep—"

"Yeh, I know. I know what you told me. Christ, a guy'd have to stay up all day *and* night to get anywhere before you." Jolly watched the car's lights swing over the top of the hill that led to his street.

"You gonna shut up a friggin' minute?" Luke asked. "Listen, I didn't really expect no—I didn't think she would the first night, fer chrissake." Luke wanted to talk about it. "Jeez, I never saw nobody as ready as —well, goddamit, Jolly, you *could* have! Anybody could have."

"Can't you ever see anything? Can't you ever see anything, or know anydamnthing?"

Luke stopped the car at Jolly's house. "You ain't makin' much sense. Know what? You act like you was saving her, or something."

"Maybe I was," Jolly said quietly, his face to the window again.

"What?"

"Nothing." The two boys were silent for a time, each watching the rain splash and spread on the glass. "Forget it. I don't give a rat's ass. Screw her all you want to. And screw you, too." Jolly breathed deeply and sat up straight, his hand on the door handle.

"You comin' with me?" Luke asked.

"No. I'm going to get out of these goddam wet clothes and eat something."

Luke laughed.

"All right, garbage-mind," Jolly grinned. "What're we going to do tonight?"

"I don't know. What d'you wanta do?"

"I don't know." Jolly opened the door and stood out into the rain. "I'll walk down in a couple of hours. Will you be through by then—with the body and all?"

“I’ll come get you, Jolly. You’ll be all wet again,” Luke said.

“No. No, I’ll wear my idiot raincoat.” Jolly shut the car door and stood with his hands in his pockets while the Blue Goose spun wildly away into the wet street.

SIXTEEN

JOLLY slammed the back door and stood scraping the soles of his shoes on the square of carpeting that lay for that purpose on the worn linoleum. "Mom?"

"In here," she answered from the living room. "Come see who I got."

He walked into the other room. "What in hell—in the world is that?" he asked.

There in the middle of the floor, seated on a folded quilt, sat a little boy playing with a hairbrush and some blocks. He looked up at the sound of Jolly's voice and laughed. Beside him in her rocker, her attention bent protectively toward him, sat Jolly's mother, beaming, but trying not to show it.

"Where'd you get *him?*" Jolly asked. The little boy laughed.

"Isn't he cute?" She bent down from the rocker to retrieve a flung block. "The spittin' image of your father."

Jolly stood dripping wet. "What are you talking about, Mother? Whose is he? Where'd you get him?"

Mattawilde leaned back in her rocker and watched the boy. "That black hair," she said. "And those eyes."

"Mother."

"He's Jamie's," she said, and her eyes flicked to Jolly's face for a moment.

"Jamie's! How do you know? Where'd he come from? Jamie's and who else's? He didn't tell me he was *married,* for crap's sake."

His mother rocked and watched the baby pound one block on another. "Those were Jamie's blocks," she said. Then she said, "Well, he isn't married. But he's about to be," she added quickly. "And you needn't tell anybody different."

Jolly sat on the sofa and then stood again and moved to a wooden chair that his wetness would not harm. "Jeez, I don't know what you're even talking about."

Jolly kicked a stray block gently back toward the edge of the quilt. "Who's the mother? And how'd he get hold of this baby if he's not married? And how did *you* get hold of it, in the first place?"

"We're going to keep him a few days while they go off on a little trip. Understand, Jolly, this isn't the right way—there's never been anything like this in my family before—but they're going to straighten things out."

"Well, where'd she come from? Who is she?"

Mattawilde's mouth tightened briefly, then relaxed again. "I don't know, for sure," she said. "I haven't met her yet. Jamie wanted things to be—better first."

"Jeez," Jolly commented.

"And you just watch yourself when the time comes, young man."

"Don't worry."

“Things will work out. Look at that hair and eyes. The spittin’ image,” she reflected.

“Yeh,” Jolly said and unconsciously touched his own blond hair. “Aren’t we going to eat?” he asked.

“Oh, Lordy,” his mother said. She heaved herself up from the chair. “I pert’ neally forgot all about supper. You run get some dry clothes and bring ’em in here to change where they’s a fire and you can keep a eye on Him.” The pronoun was deified.

“Jeez,” said Jolly. “I’m an uncle again, Granny! Wait’ll I tell Luke. He’ll never be an uncle.”

“You’re not plannin’ to go out again in this rain, are you?” Mattawilde said. She came back to the doorway from the kitchen and peered around it to see if the boy was safe.

The store lights and the neon of Whiskey Row were on in the town when Jolly crossed the plaza two hours later. The fish in the iron-railed pond were hidden from sight, resting on the bottom of their public wetness while the rain kept up a mass of constantly converging circles over their heads. Teddy Roosevelt and his green steed charged the coming night. A few people hurried from awning to awning in front of J. C. Penney’s and Sears and the dime store.

Jolly approached the Meaders Mortuary from the front, instead of from the alley as he usually did. The pillared façade rose blankly and starkly white in the gray evening. No lights shone from the windows either downstairs or upstairs, which should have been the first sign that something was different about the mortuary this night. Jolly tried the front door and found it locked. "Funny," he said. He walked around the side, ducking under the heavy-hanging willows. From near the back a blue-white light filtered through Venetian blinds, causing the rain drops to flicker as they fell. Someone was in the office. At the window Jolly could make out, in narrow horizontal strips, the back of George Meaders, apparently asleep at his desk.

He tried the next door, the one that led to the music room from the outside, and found it unlocked. Once inside he made his way cautiously to the office, guided by the blue-white neon light.

At the doorway he stopped and viewed the sleeping man at the desk. George Meaders' fingers still rested lightly on the round desk ashtray. In it a cigarette burned, a long ash bent along the inner curve of the bowl. From a half-open desk drawer the brown neck of a whiskey bottle stretched, topless. George Meaders breathed easily. Jolly wondered why Luke and Mrs. Meaders would have gone out and left him sleeping like that. But then, maybe they didn't know.

"Mr. Meaders," Jolly said.

The man made a chewing noise with his mouth and rolled his head.

"Mr. Meaders!" Jolly touched the sleeping man's shoulder.

George Meaders raised his head slowly, the gray hair hanging limply over his forehead. For a moment he seemed not to see anything but only stared over the top of his desk toward the opposite wall. Then he felt Jolly's hand on his shoulder and whirled toward him, his eyes wild and unfocused.

"Sorry to startle you, sir," Jolly said. He moved away from the desk and George Meaders' staring face. "Is Luke home? I just came by to see Luke." Jolly feigned interest in a framed magazine photograph of a blue lake set beneath a single snow-capped blue mountain.

When Mr. Meaders did not answer, Jolly turned back to him, expecting to find him asleep again. Instead, he was reaching the whiskey bottle out of the drawer, and having some difficulty doing it, and with the other hand he was holding a glass already a third full. He concentrated, tight-lipped, on the job of pouring. He was about to replace the bottle when he stopped and seemed confused. He then drew another glass from the drawer and poured it half full. He extended the glass feebly. "Here," he said. "For you."

Jolly took the glass of whiskey because he couldn't think what else to do. He watched George Meaders drink from the full glass, cough, and then swivel in his chair so that he leaned over the desk, the glass in both hands. He lifted his eyes to Jolly. They were bleary and red.

"What's the matter, Mr. Meaders? What's wrong?"

"You don't know?"

"No, sir. What should I know?"

"No. Of course you don't know. How could you."

"Please, sir. I don't know what you're talking about." Jolly felt the chill from his wet raincoat.

Luke's father drew a great shuddering breath, and it seemed to take all his strength. "Luke is dead."

Jolly watched his face and knew unquestioningly that what he had heard was true. Luke's father, suddenly more gray than before, wiped his shirt sleeve over his eyes and rested his face for a moment on the crook of his arm. Jolly felt the room pitch crazily and then come back into place. "No," he whispered. "No." He sat in a chair and saw George Meaders raise his head and search for a moment before his eyes found Jolly's again.

"How, Mr. Meaders? How?"

"Ambulance," Mr. Meaders said. "He went out on a call."

"Where?" Jolly spoke breathlessly, urgent that Mr. Meaders would hurry, would tell quickly—as if it mattered. It did matter.

Luke's father waved his hand vaguely. "Arrowhead," he said. That would be nearly fifteen miles.

"Was he alone? What happened? I thought he was going to the County to pick up a body."

"Yes, alone. The—I went for that one. No one to go—" His words disappeared in soundless sobs, and he held his hand over his eyes.

"What have they done—where is he now, Mr. Meaders? Have they brought him in?"

George Meaders removed the hand from over his eyes and ran his finger around the lip of the glass that he still held. "Andersen went out to get him. He's here."

"You mean here in the mortuary? The preparation room?"

"Yes." Luke's father continued to stare at the glass, but his eyes filled, and when he blinked the tears coursed down the creases of his face beside his nose.

Jolly looked away and fought against the lump that rose from the pit of his stomach to his throat. He watched the blue mountain until the room settled again. He said "Did you—has he been—"

"Yes. Andersen's in there now. All except the trocar. I couldn't let him." George Meaders broke down and wept openly, his head cradled on one arm, the other still reaching toward the glass of whiskey.

Jolly stood and looked at the glass he held. He set it on the desk. "Go up and go to bed, Mr. Meaders." He touched the man's arm. "Go on," he said gently. "I'll—I'll lock up down here." He met George Meaders' gaze. They stared at each other for a moment, and the old man looked relieved.

"Thank you, Jolly," Luke's father said.

Jolly watched him climb the stairs that led from the office to the floor above. He turned to see Caleb Andersen just entering the room.

"Meaders gone up?" he asked.

"Yes, sir," Jolly said. "Have you—are you—is it finished?" he asked.

Caleb Andersen reached his hat down from the coat tree. "Yes," he sighed. "Except for the trocar. He ought to let me do that. It's got to be done."

"Mr. Andersen, tell me—tell me what happened."

"It's a shame," he said. He lifted the glass of whiskey

from the desk and drank. "No goddam need for it, neither."

Jolly sat on the bottom step of the stairs and waited for Caleb Andersen to go on.

"That blond whore from Freddy's and one a her studs. They didn't even need no ambulance. Just a wrecker."

He drank again from the glass and then jammed his hat on his head. "Probably got to foolin' with him in the car and he ran off the road. Lucky. That kind's always lucky. All she got out of it was a bump on the head that'll give her a headache for a week."

Caleb Andersen set the empty glass on the desk and turned to Jolly. "Can you close up around here? I'm going. I'm sick to my stomach."

"Yes, sir," said Jolly.

Jolly walked through the chapel and the music room in the dark. He opened the door of the preparation room and felt for the light switch. The neon tubes flickered twice and then held, shedding their cold light over the room, the stretcher, the calendar girl, the blood-vessel chart, the embalming machine, the sheeted figure on the stainless steel table that could be raised or lowered or tilted like a seesaw.

Before he pulled back the sheet, Jolly took the long steel needle from its cabinet. He opened a quart jar of pink embalming fluid and turned his face from the sharp odor of formaldehyde. He screwed the needle onto the jar. He set the jar on a shelf near the head of the table. He lifted back the sheet slowly and gazed long at the umber, translucent face, grinless and calm beneath the straight black hair. Jolly pushed the hair away from Luke's face, but it settled back naturally over his eyes. He lifted it again and saw the large blue crease that dented Luke's skull, running from above his left eye to his hairline.

Farther down, as the sheet was pulled away, was the plump chest with its new black hair lying flat. Then the hands appeared just above the spot where the trocar must go, the left folded over the right, incongruously placed, the nails broken and in need of cleaning. Then came the rampant black hair again and the genitals, lying harmless and limp and lopsided. A few inches farther down was the tiny incision closed now with sutures.

Jolly chose a spot, low on the abdomen, where the sun-darkened skin gave way to a short band of lighter skin. He placed the drill-like needle exactly on that line and turned his body half away from Luke's face. The trocar pierced the flesh and sank deep. The pink liquid gurgled in the bottle.

He looked to Luke's face, half expecting to see him grimace with pain. No expression flitted across the lips, wired shut forever from the inside and sealed with wax.

"You crazy," Jolly said. "You crazy bastard moron. Probably driving a thousand miles an hour in the rain." Jolly felt his own stomach knot and then loosen and begin to jerk. "I think I'll just put your damn flowers on the wrong grave. Or better, I'll spread 'em all over the goddam road."

He changed the position of the trocar, and it waved

before his eyes as something seen in a watery mirror. "I'm laughing. See Luke? I'm doing it again, and this time you can't do a goddam thing about it. I'm laughing, Luke, I'm laughing."

The trocar gurgled again, and the pink liquid was gone.

Jolly pulled the instrument back and saw the little round hole that remained, just on the line of the dark flesh and the lighter flesh. A pale edge of liquid formed around the hole.

"You want another belly-button, Luke?" He screwed the plastic button into the hole, pressing harder than was needed. "There." The firm flesh rose slowly into place. "Now you're all sewed, sealed, and screwed." Jolly took off his glasses and ran the sleeve of his damp jacket over his eyes. "Get it, Luke? You've *really* been screwed this time, buddy. You been screwed good!"

He pulled the sheet back up. Before he covered Luke's face, he swept back the sheaf of black hair again. "And can't you keep your goddam hair combed, you crazy moron," he said.

Jolly left the preparation room with the bare neon light still burning. In the music room he stopped beside the old organ and ran his hand along its black curves. He walked on, through the chapel, into the office. The light was still on. Jolly moved with determination. He set the two glasses in the desk drawer and closed it. He opened the narrow center desk drawer and searched among its contents. Not finding what he sought, he took from it a paper clip. This he unbent into a single wire. Holding it between his teeth he bent small notches along more than an inch of it. He turned to the wooden filing cabinet and inserted the wire in the lock of the middle drawer. Carefully he twisted the wire like a miniature crank until finally it caught and the lock clicked open.

He spread open the graveyard chart on the floor. He knelt beside it and swung it around until the arrow in the bottom corner pointed north. Starting at the mausoleum, he searched west with his finger, bending low in order to read the names printed in the little oblong boxes. He found it without much trouble. OSMENT, one of the boxes read. It was just about where he thought it should be. He moved his finger back to the big center square and carefully counted the rows, the aisles, the curves in the path.

Jolly refolded the chart along its deep-creased lines and returned it to the filing cabinet. He twisted the bent wire until the lock clicked again. He flung the wire toward the wastebasket and shut off the light.

He walked through the chapel in total darkness. In the music room he cracked his shin against a chair, and the chair clattered loudly against the wall. He stopped to rub the hurt briefly, then guided by the light under the door, he re-entered the preparation room.

He found Luke's clothes piled in a heap on a chair. He lifted the pants and ran his hand into the right front pocket. He pulled out the two keys on a brass chain, decorated with a tiny black telescope through which one could see a bulbous naked woman if he held the telescope to the light. Jolly dropped the pants back onto the chair and let himself out the back door. He had carefully avoided the steel table with the body of Luke on it like some shapeless biscuit-man beneath the sheet.

The Blue Goose objected noisily, then started. Jolly backed it out of the garage and turned down the muddy alley. The rain shied across the headlights in streaks of yellow and silver. He drove through town, past where the night neon cast wavering reflections out onto the wet streets, past Rosy's Tavern that glowed warmly on the corner.

He turned onto the Shaker Village Road and drove unhurriedly past the old yellowed houses, over the bridge and the railroad tracks, into the jumbled, loud clutter of Shaker Village. There, outside the unpainted wooden fence of a wrecking yard, was the Meaders' white ambulance, its nose just lowering from the hoist of a wrecker. Jolly stopped the Blue Goose, and watched while two men in greasy overalls and caps worked in the glare from the tow-truck's spotlights. Finally, one man climbed into the truck and drove it a few feet away, then both men went through a gate in the wooden fence into the wrecking yard.

Jolly walked cautiously to the ambulance. Its white length was shortened ridiculously. He ran his hand along the smooth right side of the body, around to the other side where the metal was folded and creased and muddied. From where he stood, the hood bent upward like the broken wing of a great bird. He stopped a long time by the door on the driver's side. The door itself, in fact the whole body from frame to roof, was smashed in as if some giant-child had thrown down his toy in anger. The wheel on that side was missing entirely. Jolly wondered if it was still out there, lying wherever it had bounced to, probably down into a canyon, flinging crazily every few feet as it met another granite boulder, while above on the road Luke fought the last split second of his life against odds no human could ever match, his hands twisting at the steering wheel even after it had crushed his chest, even as his head cracked among the apparatus of the ambulance—the heavy steel bottle of oxygen, the chromium-plated bed on wheels—even as these flew murderously forward among the neatly rolled bandages, and the little jars of iodine and Merthiolate, and the square white tin box with the red cross that held all the puny contrivances for keeping people alive and their blood inside their veins a few more moments, even as the dark eyes closed part way from their wide terror and stared unblinking into the soft rain that soothed through paneless windows.

Jolly drove on, along the paved road that stretched darkly for two miles more to where the swooping granite wall began.

The graveyard seemed darker, if anything, and quieter than the rest of the night. The car's headlights swept over the rows of stones turned gray from the rain, and over the grass-warmed undulations of the earth. The pine trunks were brown in the car's lights, but the tops were unseen in the sky. Jolly saw the baskets and sprays of expensive flowers on the first graves. Most were beaten down by the rain and seemed to clutter, rather than decorate.

"I'm a day late for Memorial Day," he said.

He left the Blue Goose standing before the mausoleum. The little coupe seemed to shrink beneath the stone power of the tomb, which loomed more awesome for being only barely visible. He unhooked Luke's flashlight from the steering column and played the beam over the near gravel walks, choosing carefully. The light made an elongated circle directly before his feet as he walked, counting the squares, the paths. He no longer felt the rain on his clothes or the cold that had come with darkness.

He stopped. He shined the light over a mound and remembered it as the unmarked grave on which he had cast his bouquet of nasturtiums long ago. The weeds still ranged over it, no better or worse than they had before. No holiday flowers decorated it.

He stared a long time at the grave, wondering why he was there and why he felt nothing in particular now that he knew for sure. He kicked idly at the weeds along the edge of the loaf of earth. The bright beam of the flashlight, cutting against the black, made him dizzy. His mind passed over the days just gone, jumbling the events in a meaningless whirl. His thoughts came back to Luke lying snugly dead on the steel table that tilted like a seesaw. Jolly felt himself say "Luke is dead" for the first time.

He kicked at the weeds. They were old and tough and resisted the kicks despite the wetness of the earth. "Goddamit!" he said aloud. "Goddam, goddam."

The weeds bent and some began to tear loose, their roots gouging out clumps of dirt as they toppled. Jolly kicked harder with the toe of his shoe, and it would have been difficult to say if his face was wet with tears or rain.

Suddenly, near the head of the mound, he kicked, and the edge of a tin marker pointed from the earth. He bent down slowly and pulled it the rest of the way out. He squatted, and turning the isinglass side up, he rubbed it. When most of the mud was gone he held it out to the rain until the surface was clean.

Holding the flashlight in one hand and the marker in the other, by its single long spiked leg, he drew it close to his face to read it. There was nothing on it. The writing had faded, and the only signs that there had ever been writing were the little pale rivulets of blue permanently stained on the paper around the edges.

Jolly stood with the tin marker in his hands.

A deep breath, one of those that come without warning, passed through his chest, causing him to straighten abruptly. The rain washed down over his hair and face and ran in tiny streams down the back of his neck and, it seemed, all over his body.

The marker fell silently into the wet earth, spear first, and sank deep. With his foot Jolly drove the square slice of tin down into the grave until nothing showed of it but a narrow strip at the top, even with the ground.

He clicked off the light. While his eyes adjusted

to the deeper blackness, he faced the rain and let it wash.

After a time he walked back toward the Blue Goose standing beneath the faceless tower of gray stone. He walked without the light, watching the pebble paths curve beneath his feet.

The other car was parked behind the Blue Goose. It was some dark color—maroon or maybe black—but it would have been impossible to say which, parked the way it was in the wet shadow of night. Only the dim circles of its white-walled tires told where the car and the road separated.

The man leaned against the smaller car, his coat collar turned up against the rain, shielding the lighted cigarette in his cupped hand. As Jolly approached, the orange pin of light skittered onto the road and was instantly killed by the rain.

"Did you find it?"

Jolly stopped, confused. Then he saw the man. He knew the voice.

"How did you know—"

"Never mind." Jolly felt the hands touch his face on either side. "I know," the voice said. "I know."

EPILOGUE

Now, therefore, while the youthful hue
Sits on thy skin like morning dew,
And while thy willing soul transpires
At every pore with instant fires,
Now let us sport us while we may;
And now, like amorous birds of prey,
Rather at once our Time devour,
Than languish in his slow-chapt power.
Let us roll all our strength and all
Our sweetness up into one ball,
And tear our pleasures with rough strife
Thorough the iron gates of life.
Thus, though we cannot make our Sun
Stand still, yet we will make him run.

—Andrew Marvell